• Word arou_____ ___ _e
mailman and ___ _____ __ared quite
the romantic n_____ ___ they were
trapped togethe___ __e elevator during a
blackout. But reliable sources say that Mike
has been keeping a million-dollar secret that,
once known, is sure to surprise everybody—
most especially Sophia!

• Good things really do come in small
packages. Congratulations to Olivia and
Lucas Hunter on the birth of their son,
Nathaniel Wyatt Hunter!

• Finally, did you hear the news? It seems
as if Rex Barrington II is destined for a
romance of his own. We all know that his
faithful assistant, Mildred Van Hess, has
stood by the company president for
years...but rumors abound that it was
because of more than just professional
loyalty!

Dear Reader,

In May 2000 Silhouette Romance will commemorate its twentieth anniversary! This line has always celebrated the essence of true love in a manner that blends classic themes and the challenges of romance in today's world into a reassuring, fulfilling novel. From the enchantment of first love to the wonder of second chance, a Silhouette Romance novel demonstrates the power of genuine emotion and the breathless connection that develops between a man and a woman as they discover each other. And this month's stellar selections are quintessential Silhouette Romance stories!

If you've been following LOVING THE BOSS, you'll be amazed when mysterious Rex Barrington III is unmasked in *I Married the Boss!* by Laura Anthony. In this month's FABULOUS FATHERS offering by Donna Clayton, a woman discovers *His Ten-Year-Old Secret.* And opposites attract in *The Rancher and the Heiress,* the third of Susan Meier's TEXAS FAMILY TIES miniseries.

WRANGLERS & LACE returns with Julianna Morris's *The Marriage Stampede.* In this appealing story, a cowgirl butts heads—and hearts—with a bachelor bent on staying that way. Sally Carleen unveils the first book in her exciting duo ON THE WAY TO A WEDDING… with the tale of a twin mistaken for an M.D.'s *Bride in Waiting!* It's both a blessing and a dilemma for a single mother when she's confronted with an amnesiac *Husband Found,* this month's FAMILY MATTERS title by Martha Shields.

Enjoy the timeless power of Romance this month, and every month—you won't be disappointed!

Mary-Theresa Hussey

Mary-Theresa Hussey
Senior Editor, Silhouette Romance

Please address questions and book requests to:
Silhouette Reader Service
U.S.: 3010 Walden Ave., P.O. Box 1325, Buffalo, NY 14269
Canadian: P.O. Box 609, Fort Erie, Ont. L2A 5X3

I MARRIED THE BOSS!

Laura Anthony

Silhouette

ROMANCE™

Published by Silhouette Books

America's Publisher of Contemporary Romance

Special thanks and acknowledgment are given to
Laurie Blalock Vanzura, writing as Laura Anthony, for
her contribution to the *Loving the Boss* miniseries.

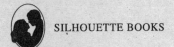 SILHOUETTE BOOKS

ISBN 0-373-19372-6

I MARRIED THE BOSS!

Copyright © 1999 by Harlequin Books S.A.

Look us up on-line at: http://www.romance.net

Printed in U.S.A.

LAURA ANTHONY

started writing at age eight. She credits her father, Fred Blalock, as the guiding force behind her career. Although a registered nurse, Laura has achieved a life-long dream and now pursues writing fiction full time. Her hobbies include jogging, boating, traveling and reading voraciously.

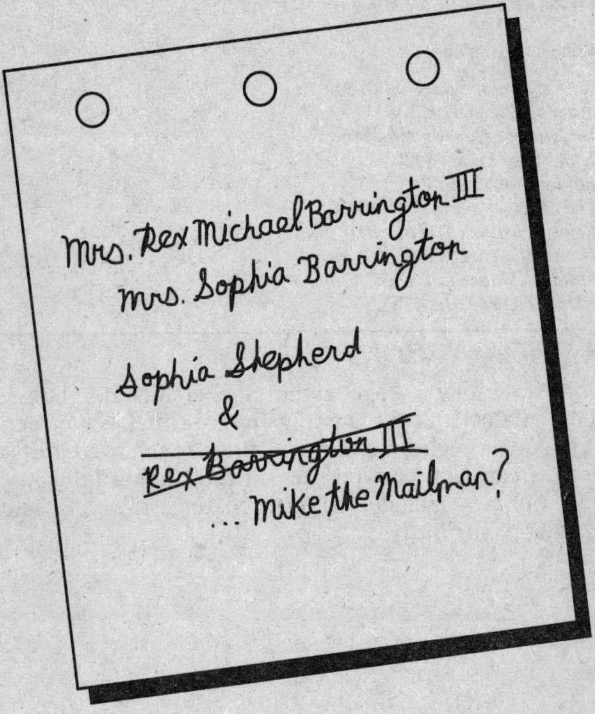
Mrs. Rex Michael Barrington III
Mrs. Sophia Barrington
Sophia Shepherd
&
~~Rex Barrington III~~
... Mike the Mailman?

Chapter One

Mrs. Rex Michael Barrington III.

Sophia Shepherd doodled across the yellow legal notepad and gave a heartfelt sigh. Four months into her new job as assistant to the executive vice president of the Barrington Corporation and she had yet to even meet her boss, much less achieve her goal of marrying him. In fact, she knew very little about the man beyond his sexy telephone voice and his sharp business acumen.

Mrs. Sophia Barrington.

The fact that her five best girlfriends, Cindy, Olivia, Molly, Rachel and Patricia, had all fallen in love with their bosses had set Sophia's imagination into overdrive. Could she, too, marry her boss? After all, love was definitely in the air. Olivia had already wed Lucas Hunter and Cindy was due to walk down the aisle with Kyle Prentice in November. Was it too much to hope that some of that magical stardust might one day settle upon her, bringing into her life the same profound happiness her friends had discovered? Of course, her five friends had a distinct advantage over her. They'd actually known their bosses while Sophia had a crush on a man she'd never even seen.

Yet, she and her boss talked on the phone daily, and Mr. Barrington—although Sophia liked to think of him as Michael so as not to confuse him with his father, Rex Michael Barrington II—often praised her efficiency. Surely she hadn't imagined the admiration in his voice last week when he'd told her that she was the best assistant he'd ever had and that when he arrived in Phoenix to take over the family business after his father retired in two months, he intended on treating her to dinner?

Dinner with Michael Barrington? Sophia's toes curled at the prospect. She couldn't have been more excited if Tom Cruise himself had asked her for a date.

Dreamily Sophia closed her eyes and allowed her reverie full rein. They'd dine at Reflections in the White Swan Hotel in Sedona, the most exclusive restaurant in the most exclusive vacation chain owned by the Barrington Corporation. They'd drink Dom Pérignon, nibble on turkey medallions marinated in mushroom wine sauce and have cherries jubilee for dessert.

Afterward, Michael would invite her for a late-night stroll along the lake. Demurely she would agree. They'd step outside into the warm night air. He'd take her hand. His grip would be strong and comforting. They would walk for several minutes, his sexy voice rolling over her like heated body oil. The moon would be bright and full, bathing them in an ethereal glow. Michael would tell her how much he admired her work and how much he trusted her as his personal secretary. Sophia would respond in kind, telling him he was the most industrious, responsible, empowering boss she'd ever worked for.

Michael would stop and gently draw her into the curve of his arm. His heavenly smell, an expensive men's cologne, would intoxicate her senses. She'd catch her breath and look up into those dark eyes. Sophia liked to pretend that he possessed eyes as deep brown as a Hershey's Chocolate Kiss.

"Sophia." Michael would whisper her name in that throaty baritone of his and she would tumble helplessly under his spell. "I can't tell you how much you've come to mean to me over the past few months."

"But, Michael," she would protest, but ever so slightly, "we've only just met face-to-face."

"That's not important," he would argue. "And although you are an attractive woman, your looks are of no consequence. I've come to know the real you over the phone and through your funny little faxes and your witty e-mail messages. I trust you, Sophia Shepherd. Truly, deeply, as I've never trusted another."

"Oh, Michael." She would sigh and he'd sweep her against his chest. His lips would come down on hers in a haunting, soul-searching kiss. A tender kiss that would make her feel comfortable, safe and secure. A kiss that held promises of happily-ever-after.

"Good morning, Sophia."

Ripped from her delicious daydream, Sophia jerked her attention to the doorway.

Mike Barr, the office mailman, lounged seductively against the doorjamb, his hips cocked forward in a nonchalant slouch, a come-hither grin curling the corners of his lips and a daring twinkle sparking in his green eyes. His dark brown hair was sexily mussed as if he hadn't bothered with a comb, had instead merely raked his fingers through it. He wore tan chinos and a crisp white polo shirt which did nothing to camouflage his tanned muscular forearms.

He possessed a voice almost as deep as her boss's, but where Michael Barrington spoke in a commanding rush, Mike, the office mailman, let words drip off his tongue like heated molasses, and he dished up compliments as readily as he handed out the company mail.

Despite her best intentions to the contrary, Sophia experienced a hot rush of desire instantly replace the lingering sweetness of her fantasy. Darn it! What was it about this particular man that so stirred her blood?

"Good morning, Mike," Sophia replied evenly, refusing to give him a clue to the unrestrained chemistry ramming through her whenever she looked at him. The man need never know that although her heart belonged to Michael Barrington, her fickle body seemed to prefer the mailman's outdoorsy good looks.

Sure, Mike was the sexiest thing on two legs. Nobody could deny that. But when a girl looked at him, what she saw was what she got. A handsome guy at the bottom of the corporate ladder with no ambitions to climb higher. A guy who might be great for a few weeks of carefree adventure but one who would certainly falter when it came to long-term commitment. A guy who was here one minute and gone the next with nary a serious thought for what the future might hold.

No, Sophia could not afford to let Mike know that she found him physically attractive. Because that's all it was, she assured herself. Physical attraction. Erotic sensations founded on lust. What she felt for Mike was the exact opposite of her feelings for Michael Barrington. Now there was a guy you could count on. Harvard graduate, hardworking, energetic, take-charge, absolutely nothing like the lackadaisical, "play-today-don't-worry-about-tomorrow," Mike. It reminded her of the old fable of the ant and the grasshopper. Michael was the ant, Mike the grasshopper. With the grasshopper you might have a heady summer filled with fun but come winter you'd starve to death, and Sophia had experienced more than enough lean winters in her life, thank you very much.

"You're looking mighty fine this morning, Miss Sophia," Mike drawled lazily, his steady gaze flicking over her as hot and dry as the bright Arizona sunshine swelling through the mauve miniblinds and flooding the carpet with dappled lighting.

"Thank you," she replied, casually placing a file over the damning legal pad in front of her. She was nervous that Mike might spy the doodlings and find out about her secret crush on her boss. She could not risk an office scandal. "What can I do for you?" she said.

His grin widened and instantly Sophia realized her poor choice of words.

"The question is, what can I do for you?" He moved across the room, lethal as a leopard, his smooth movements so mesmerizing, she barely noticed the brown paper package cradled loosely in the crook of his arm.

"Excuse me?" Gulping, she stared, her eyes transfixed on his broad chest. Whenever he loped into the room it was as if her brain flew straight out the window.

"I brought something for you." Mike extended the package toward Sophia.

"Oh?" She accepted it and with her utility scissors snipped away the string. The package had her name on it but there was no return address. Odd. It had been mailed in Phoenix and postmarked the previous day.

Mike stayed. Boldly watching her.

"Is there something else?"

Sophia looked up as she asked the question, and to her dismay, couldn't prevent her gaze from crashing into his, resulting in the mental equivalent of a five-car pileup. The man was brash and sexy and dangerous. If she weren't careful, her heart could end up as so much carnage on the emotional highway of runaway lust. For that very reason, she had always avoided entanglements with men like him. She refused to be swayed by the romantic notion of the bad boy cured by a good woman's love. She knew that fatal attraction for what it was. A perilous myth.

Mike's eyes crinkled at the corners. "I thought you might have some outgoing mail."

But Sophia recognized a stalling technique when she saw one. Mike was snooping, waiting to see what the package held.

"I suppose you could take what I've already accumulated but I'll have more after lunch." She waved a hand at the stack of envelopes resting in the mail bin.

"I'll take these off your hands for now, then I'll come back later for the rest," he said.

"All right."

Cripes! Why did her body break out in tingly patches at the prospect of seeing him again today?

"Speaking of lunch," he said, "I was wondering..."

Please, don't let him ask me out, she prayed, terrified that her body would not allow her mind to refuse his invitation.

"If you'd like to grab a bite to eat with me," he finished, confirming her worst fear.

"I don't think so." Sophia shook her head. "But thank you for asking." Purposefully she returned her attention to the computer screen, signaling that the conversation had ended. Mike did not take the hint.

"May I ask you a personal question?"

"If I'm not obligated to answer it."

His grin widened. "Fair enough."

She gazed at him expectantly. "What's your burning question?"

"Are you seeing anyone? I've asked around the office and no one seems to know. You're quite secretive about your private life, Sophia Shepherd. Are you hiding a mystery man?"

That's because she didn't have a private life!

"No mystery." She smiled gently, not wanting to hurt his feelings with a blunt rejection. He was a nice enough guy, even if he wasn't her type. "I simply keep myself very busy."

She swung her arm around to take another crack at unwrapping the package and to keep her eyes off Mike. Her finger caught the edge of the manila folder hiding her doodles. The folder skittered across the desk and landed on the floor.

"I'll get that for you," Mike said.

"No, don't bother."

Quickly she jumped up and hurried around the desk, anxious to prevent him from seeing the embarrassing writing, but Sophia was too slow.

Mike scooped the folder from the floor and returned it to her desk. She saw one eyebrow arch as he leaned over, cocked his head and read what was scrawled on the notepad. She crossed her arms over her chest and stared pointedly at the calendar on her wall. She paid an inordinate amount of attention to the picture of an inquisitive Siamese kitten in a basket of red yarn, while vainly attempting to stay the heated flush zipping across her cheeks.

Without saying a word, Mike retrieved the letters from the mail bin. He strolled toward the door, then hesitated before stepping over the threshold. He cast a backward glance over his shoulder at her.

"Be careful what you wish for, Miss Sophia," he cautioned. "You just might get it."

What did he mean by that? Sophia wondered in irritation. She watched his back as he sauntered away, helplessly noticing how well his chinos cupped his firm behind.

"Forget Mike," she mumbled.

Sophia went back to her desk, sat down and returned her attention to the strange package. The brown paper crinkled in her hands. She picked up her scissors again and sliced through to the cardboard box underneath. It was wrapped in festive birthday paper. Sophia smiled. This morning, her mother had given her a birthday card and the crimson scarf she now wore knotted about her neck, but no one else in the building had wished her a happy birthday. Clearly one of her friends had remembered the date even though she made a point to keep her birthday a secret. Sophia had never cared for parties or fanfare.

Twenty-nine. Technically an old maid. She had always figured she'd be married by age twenty-nine with a baby or two. Unfortunately she'd never met a man she could truly believe in. An honest man who could provide the secure stable life she'd always craved. A man who would not lie to her the way her father had once lied to her mother. A good-hearted man committed to his family and his career.

In Sophia's experience there weren't many such men in the world. Most guys resembled Mike the mailman, overgrown boys looking for someone to take care of them while they ran around having a good time. But if she had her way, by this time next year she would be Mrs. Rex Michael Barrington III and have a baby on the way.

Sophia removed the rest of the wrapping paper and opened the box. It contained a glass paperweight carved in the shape of a gray, sloe-eyed kitten. How sweet! Someone knew how much she adored kittens. Which of her friends had sent it? Was it Patricia? She had access to personnel records and could easily uncover Sophia's birth date. Curiously she peered inside the empty box but did not find a card with the name of the sender.

Turning the paperweight over in her hand, Sophia admired the smooth lines. She saw an inscription on the bottom which read To The World's Greatest Secretary. Happy Birthday.

Her heart gave an erratic thump, and euphoria, brilliant

as a rainbow, splashed through her. Blood rushed to her head and her skin prickled. Michael had not only taken the trouble to discover when her birthday was but he'd sent a present, as well! Sophia was so touched by the thoughtful gesture, her eyes misted and a lump rose to her throat.

And it was postmarked from Phoenix.

Sophia caught her breath. That could only mean one thing.

Michael Barrington had come home!

Excited, she leapt from her chair and clutching the precious paperweight in her hand, tore down the hallway after Mike.

Why had seeing *Mrs. Rex Michael Barrington III* scribbled over Sophia's notepad affected him so strongly? Mike shook his head. He supposed it was because he'd thought she was different, but it seemed Sophia Shepherd was as shallow as all the other women he'd ever known. Fortune hunters, interested not in the size of a man's heart, but only in the size of his wallet.

Disheartened, he stepped into the elevator and pressed the button for the basement floor which housed the mail room. Sophia's letters were still in his hand. The paper smelled of her perfume. Something fresh and floral. Wildflowers. Sweet, bright and full of sunshine. Mike raised the envelopes to his nose and inhaled deeply before tucking them securely into his back pocket.

Normally he was very self-confident when it came to dealing with women, but whenever he got around Sophia, he felt like an inept birdbrain. He fumbled, he stumbled, he stuck his foot in his mouth and said things he didn't mean. Mike sighed. He shouldn't allow himself to go gaga over her. A woman as beautiful as Sophia could never be interested in just a guy from the mail room.

Unfortunately.

Mike shrugged aside the disappointment surging through his stomach. He'd expected so much more from her. Hell, he'd hoped… Yes, stupidly, he'd hoped. He knew the way the world really worked. Had known for most of his thirty-six years. Even though Sophia was attracted to him, the doodling on her notepad was proof enough. Sophia Shepherd was angling to land herself a millionaire. A millionaire she'd never even met. Obviously it didn't matter to her what kind of person Rex Michael Barrington III was, only that he possessed a large bank account.

The elevator door slid open. Head down, Mike stepped out and strolled through the corridor toward the mail room. Behind him, he heard the second elevator give a muted ping as it, too, opened at the basement level.

"Mike!"

He stopped, turned.

Breathlessly Sophia dashed after him, calling his name and waving her hand. The bangle bracelets at her wrist jangled merrily. "Mike, please wait up."

He tried to deny the kick of excitement that rushed through him at the sight of her flushed face but could not. Sophia's curly, shoulder-length blond hair ruffled lightly against her high cheekbones. Her blue eyes glowed with a provocative inner light. The silky material of her white blouse gently accentuated the curve of her breasts, and the red skirt that rested two inches above her knees showcased her exquisitely shaped legs. She wore a soft red scarf knotted jauntily at her neck, which gave her the coy appearance of a 1950s movie star.

Hope rose anew. Perhaps he'd misjudged her. Maybe she'd come to take him up on his offer of lunch. Maybe she wasn't above dating the office mailman after all.

"Mike," she said, holding a glass cat in her palm. "Where did this come from?"

"I...uh..." Had she guessed already? "What is it?"

"This was in the package you brought me."

"Is there something wrong?"

"No. There's nothing wrong."

"What's the matter? Don't you like it?"

"Of course I like it." Her eyes danced.

Mike's spirits soared. He'd pleased her! "Are you sure?"

"How could I not like it?" She breathed. "Michael Barrington sent it to me."

Oh. So that's what she thought. Mike felt his face muscles sag. They were standing to one side of the passageway, a half-dozen feet from the frosted glass door of the mail room. The corridor lights cast a pale shadow over Sophia, highlighting her cheekbones, enhancing the shining glow in her eyes.

"When you got here this morning, where was the package located?" she inquired, oblivious to his fresh disappointment.

"In the mailbag. The box was brought in overnight from the post office."

"But there was no return address on it." Sophia chattered on, shredding his hopes with her unbridled enthusiasm for her absent boss. "Yet the package was postmarked from Phoenix. That means Michael is in town, doesn't it?"

"Are you sure 'the Third' sent it to you?" Mike asked, referring to the mystery man that no one in the office had ever seen but whom everyone seemed to be enamored of. That confirmed Mike's long-held conviction that rich men were always more popular than poor ones.

"What do you mean?" Sophia's brow furrowed. "Of course he sent it to me."

"You said there was no return address. Did you find a card from him inside the package?"

Slowly Sophia shook her head. "No, but read the inscription." She turned the cat over and thrust it under his nose.

But Mike didn't have to read it, he knew what had been inscribed there.

"Maybe somebody else might think you're a good secretary. Could be the big boss, Rex Barrington II himself," Mike ventured, wanting—no, aching—to take her into his arms and kiss those lips. Lips that undoubtedly tasted better than ripe strawberries and chilled champagne.

Foolish move, Mike, he mentally chided himself. Sophia doesn't want you. This girl is only interested in Michael Barrington and all that his name connotes. Money. Fame. Fortune.

"Rex Barrington has never given me anything on my birthday before," she said. "Why would he start now? But if it's not him or Michael, who could it be?"

"Just about anybody."

"Like whom?"

"Me, for instance." Mike kept talking even when it would have been prudent to shut up. "I think you're a terrific secretary, Sophia. Believe me, I do get around this building. I know who's efficient at their job and who's not."

"You?" she whispered, her blue eyes rounding in surprise. "You sent me the paperweight?"

He shrugged.

"I don't get it." She hitched in a sharp breath.

"What's to get?"

"Why would you send me a present?"

"It's your birthday and I know how much you like cats."

"How did you know it was my birthday?" she asked. "I don't make a point of announcing it."

"A little bird told me."

"You had no right to give me a present." Sophia spoke harshly, stunning Mike with her strong reaction. He had thought she would be pleased with the gift.

"I..."

"No right at all."

She blinked. Was she crying? Mike felt like a heel. He hadn't intended on hurting her.

"Sophia..." He reached out to her.

"Just forget it," she snapped, and shied from his touch.

What was she so angry about? Mike frowned. Now it was his turn to feel hurt. "Fine. If you don't like the paperweight then pitch the damn thing in the trash."

"You wanted me to think Michael Barrington sent it to me, didn't you?" Her slender fingers curled around the glass cat she held clinched at her side.

"No." *Yes.*

A furious expression lined her face. Her eyes shot liquid fire. Her mouth was screwed up into a tight pucker.

"You're a jerk, you know that."

"But you want me," Mike heard himself say even though he regretted the words before they were out of his mouth. He was proving her contention that he was a jerk, and yet he couldn't seem to halt himself. "Admit it. You're pining away for your boss because he's got money, but I'm the one who really turns you on."

"In your dreams, *mailman.*"

That one word, spoken with such disdain, did it. Before he knew what he was planning, Mike firmly grasped Sophia's shoulder with one hand and tilted her chin upward with the other.

He lowered his head until his lips were a hairbreadth

from hers. Her chest rose and fell in self-righteous indignation, but oddly enough she did not pull away.

Their breathing came in unison, hot and heavy.

Sophia stared at him, torn between slapping his presumptuous face and raising her lips for him to kiss. A thrill shot through her, humming against her nerve endings with amazing intensity. The way his hand cradled her chin, the manner in which his fingers gripped her shoulder, stirred passions inside Sophia she'd never known were there. Passions that had no place in her logical, well-ordered life.

Mike was right. She did want him. At least her body did. And that realization brought twin wheels of shame to her cheeks.

More than anyone she knew the price of unchecked passion. Her own mother had paid that dear fee and it was a price too exorbitant for any woman to pay.

How could she be so attracted to this lean muscled male when her heart truly belonged to Michael Barrington? How could her own body betray her this way?

But despite her inner protests, she could not deny that she longed to feel Mike's lips pressed to hers, heated and demanding. To feel his tongue glide along her mouth. To experience the movement of his body against hers. He would be an accomplished lover—Sophia had no doubts about his prowess.

Everyone in the office knew Mike had a way with women. He attracted members of the opposite sex the way clover attracted honeybees. He possessed that bad-boy persona that women adored. He was a rambler, a rover, a wanderer. He could show you a good time but little else. It was rumored around the office that he stayed out late and frequently attended wild parties. He rode a Harley-Davidson to work for heaven's sake and was even now wearing ankle-length leather boots.

He was the epitome of everything her mother had been warning her against for the past twenty-nine years.

And still she wanted him. With a need so strong, Sophia could taste the metallic mustiness of her passion.

His green eyes drilled into her like piercing spikes, angling down deep into her soul. Sophia sucked in air.

Think about Michael Barrington, she ordered herself.

Except she seemed unable to focus on anything except for the visage of the man before her. Michael Barrington wasn't here. Mike was. It wasn't Michael's lips promising a glimpse of undreamed of pleasure. It wasn't Michael's fingers igniting her skin nor was it Michael who had remembered her birthday.

It was Mike. The office mailman. A man with no future and no ambition. Mike, the self-professed rolling stone.

Think about your father.

That thought had the effect of ice water thrown down her back. Sophia gulped and blinked up at Mike, the spell he'd spun broken by unhappy memories.

"Let go of me," she said firmly.

Instantly Mike took his hands off her and stepped back as if released from a hypnotic spell of his own.

"I...I'm sorry," he apologized huskily. "I never should have touched you."

"Apology accepted," she whispered, knowing she was as much to blame as Mike. She should have made it perfectly clear from the very beginning that she wasn't available.

"I didn't mean to offend you, Sophia. I just wanted to give you something nice for your birthday."

"It was a sweet thought. I didn't mean to snap at you. I guess I was just disappointed."

"Disappointed that the gift was from me and not from Michael Barrington?"

She nodded wordlessly. Darn it, why was he suddenly

being so understanding? She wanted to dislike him. It would make turning him down so much easier. On legs shaky as a newborn colt's, Sophia turned and stumbled away, the gray glass cat still clutched in her hand, a talisman of frayed daydreams and hungry passions that had to be ignored.

Chapter Two

"Chemistry," Olivia McGovern Hunter, one of Sophia's closest friends, replied when Sophia finished telling her the story of what had transpired between her and Mike in the basement corridor.

They were sitting in the employee lounge on their lunch break, snacking on wedges of mozzarella cheese melted atop whole wheat crackers, with crisp apple slices on the side.

The break room, large and airy, was Sophia's favorite spot in the whole building. The floor tiles were done in the deep salmon color of an Arizona sunset and the walls were pure white. The chairs were sky blue and several strategically placed potted plants accentuated the clean decor. Although there was an outdoor dining area with redwood tables just beyond the double glass doors, the late-August heat prevented the two women from venturing beyond the air-conditioning.

"But I don't want chemistry," Sophia protested vehemently. "It's too chaotic."

"Tell me about it." Olivia grinned. "Chemistry will get you into trouble every time."

Affectionately Olivia stroked her expanded belly. She was due to deliver her first baby in less than a month and would be taking maternity leave by the end of the week. Sophia felt a twinge of sadness. She would miss her friend's sensible advice.

Sophia eyed Olivia nervously. An unplanned pregnancy was exactly the reason Sophia was determined to stay far away from passion. Olivia had been lucky in that respect. Although Olivia hadn't been married when she'd gotten pregnant, the baby's father, Lucas Hunter, had been a stand-up guy who believed in doing the right thing. Plus, Olivia and Lucas had much more going for them than mere chemistry. They were crazy in love with each other. Their adoration was easy to see.

"I'd rather have things nice and comfortable. I'll take solid and dependable over chemistry any day," Sophia declared.

"I used to think like that," Olivia said with a faraway expression in her eyes. "Until Lucas. He changed my whole outlook on life. He showed me the awesome power of true love. Trust me on this, Sophia, love beats stability any day."

"But I'm determined to make Michael Barrington fall in love with me," Sophia whispered, glancing around to make sure they were the only ones in the room. They'd taken an early lunch and the rest of the office had yet to descend upon the employee lounge. "I intend to have both chemistry and security."

"Sophia," Olivia chided, "you can't make someone fall in love with you."

"Well, he might already be in love with me," she said defensively. "You don't know that he's not."

"You've never even laid eyes on the man," Olivia

pointed out, delicately nibbling a cracker. "What if he's…well…rather unattractive?"

"I don't care what he looks like," Sophia replied. "I love him for his personality, not for his looks. Olivia, you should see some of the sweet e-mail messages he sends. He's considerate and hardworking, kind and devoted to his job."

"And in the two years you've worked here have you ever seen him around?"

"No."

"That's because this company is the most important thing in his life. Stanley Whitcomb told me Michael has been in Germany for ten years and almost never comes home to see his father. Not even for the holidays. Now, honestly, Sophia, would you really want a man like that?"

"I need someone that I know can take care of me," Sophia admitted. "A man who can assume responsibility for paying the bills. I can't end up like my mother. I won't!"

"Okay." Olivia spread her hands. "Let's say you did marry Michael Barrington. How are you going to feel five or ten years down the road when you're raising the kids by yourself? Oh sure, you're living in the lap of luxury. Big house, fancy car, all the jewelry you can wear, but where's your husband? At the office. Or on a plane. Or in some foreign country closing the next deal. Always on the go. Always working."

Sophia crinkled her nose. "It doesn't have to be like that."

"Be careful what you wish for." Olivia shook a knowing finger. "You just might get it."

"You're the second person who's said that to me today," she said, glumly thinking of Mike.

"Remember, Sophia, you deserve the best life has to offer, and that includes a man who loves you. A man who will be your lover, your confidant, your friend. You deserve what I have found with Lucas. Not just a fat wallet, or some disembodied voice over the telephone, but a real-life partner.''

''I can make him love me like that,'' Sophia insisted, raising her voice to emphasize her resolve. ''One way or another, I am going to marry Michael Barrington.''

As fate would have it, Mike the mailman picked that exact moment to walk into the break room. Sophia's words bounced off the walls. She cringed.

Without a sound, Mike headed for the coffeepot. For what seemed like an eternity he puttered with sugar and creamer, opening packets, stirring his coffee.

Had he heard her? It was one thing for him to see the doodling on her notepad. That might mean she was just a silly romantic. But to have him hear her declaring she was going to marry Michael Barrington, well that was a different matter entirely. What if he spread the gossip around the office? What if it got back to Michael himself?

Olivia stared at Sophia, her eyes wide. No one spoke.

The refrigerator door whispered open. Nibbling her bottom lip, Sophia finally dared to peek around at Mike. He was rummaging in the refrigerator, his unbelievably cute backside wagging in the air as he bent over.

Glancing at her watch, Olivia cleared her throat. ''I've got to go, Soph. My break is over.''

Panicked at the thought of being left alone in the room with Mike, Sophia clamped a hand on Olivia's arm. ''Please don't go,'' she mouthed silently.

Olivia hesitated.

Sophia placed her palms together in imitation of a prayer.

Her friend nodded.

Mike plucked a brown paper bag from the refrigerator and strolled across the break room toward them. Did the man ever move in a hurry? she wondered. He moved with the casual nonchalance of a man who had no worries, nor obligations or pressing deadlines. A man at ease in his own skin. He took the chair nearest Sophia, turned it around backward and straddled it.

Helplessly, Sophia's eyes were drawn to his powerful thighs rippling beneath the material of his tan chinos. Unbidden, she imagined those thighs completely unclothed and wrapped around her waist. Yikes! She needed an icicle shower.

"Ladies." He nodded.

"Hi, Mike," Olivia said.

"When's the little one due?" he asked, shaking his head in the direction of her expanded tummy.

Olivia smiled and circled her abdomen with both arms. "Three and a half weeks and counting."

"And Lucas is still making you work?" Mike pulled a sandwich from his paper sack.

"Oh, no," Olivia said. "Lucas wanted me to quit months ago but I promised Mr. Whitcomb I'd get everything in order for the end of the fiscal year. But Friday is my last day."

"So," Mike said, focusing all of his attention on Olivia and virtually ignoring Sophia, "do you know whether the baby is going to be a boy or a girl?"

Olivia blushed demurely. "We asked the doctor not to tell us the results of the sonogram. We want to be surprised."

Mike nodded his approval. "That's a good old-fashioned attitude. Congratulations to you and Lucas."

"Thank you." Olivia beamed.

Sophia let out a sigh. Mike had charmed another one—hook, line and sinker.

"I'll talk to you later, Sophia. I've got to be getting back." Slowly Olivia pushed herself up from the table.

She reached to pick up the cellophane wrapper from her lunch.

"Leave it." Mike waved her away with his hand. "I'll clean up."

"How thoughtful of you." Olivia smiled at him, then threw Sophia a glance that said "Give the guy a chance."

"I've got to be going, too." Sophia pushed back her chair. It scraped loudly across the tile. She picked up the remains of her lunch and noticed Mike didn't offer to clean up her mess.

"Have a nice afternoon, ladies," he drawled.

"You, too, Mike." Olivia wriggled her fingers at him.

Mike watched them leave, his complete attention focused on Sophia. He appreciated the way her hips swayed beneath that tight red skirt and the manner in which her curly blond hair bounced about her shoulders. Then, for some illogical reason he found himself wondering what Sophia would look like in Olivia's delicate condition. Would she be one of those women who carried their babies low in front? Slender except for that jut of a basketball? Would she glow with the brightness of impending motherhood the way her friend Olivia did?

"What in the hell are you thinking?" he growled to himself under his breath. Mike unwrapped his peanut butter and grape jelly sandwich but somehow lunch had lost its appeal. Darn Sophia Shepherd and her sexy ways! She had him thinking dangerous thoughts that were best not entertained.

Especially since what he'd overheard when he first came into the room had confirmed his worst fears about her. Sophia had been pledging to Olivia that she was going to make Rex Michael Barrington III fall in love with her!

Mike stared at his sandwich, trying hard to ignore the knot in his throat. The large-faced clock over the door hit twelve noon and people started arriving in the break room, laughing and joking together. He returned their greetings absentmindedly, his thoughts on Sophia and what he must do about her.

He took a bite of his sandwich and chewed pensively. So, she was determined to marry her boss. A man she'd never even seen. How could she be in love with him? There was only one explanation. She wanted to marry Michael Barrington for his money.

He took a sip of his coffee now gone tepid, and winced. But she was attracted to *him,* dammit. Mike knew he wasn't wrong about that. There was no mistaking that hungry look in her blue eyes when he'd almost kissed her in the basement corridor that morning. No denying the tremor that had run through her body when he touched her. No ignoring the sharp current of sexual electricity coursing between them.

What would she do, he wondered, when she discovered that Rex Michael Barrington III was none other than Mike Barr, office mailman? What would be her reaction then?

Mike snorted. He'd bet anything Sophia would suddenly change her tune about dating Mike.

Maybe going undercover in his father's company had not been such a great idea. Eight months ago it had seemed like the smart thing to do before Dad retired and he took over as president. Since he'd been in Germany for the past ten years setting up and running the European division of the Barrington Corporation, not many employees even knew what he looked like. It had been quite simple posing as the office mailman, and it had given him an insider's view of the company that he would not have been privy to any other way.

So far, it had been an eye-opening experience, although not always a comfortable one. He'd caught one employee stealing and another selling trade secrets to their competitors. Based on the information he'd obtained as Mike the mailman, his father Rex had fired both employees. While the charade had worked well, Michael couldn't help but feel a little underhanded about the whole thing.

And now there was this business with Sophia.

When he'd asked Patricia Peel to name Sophia as his assistant, he'd honestly chosen her for her exceptional secretarial skills. But it hadn't taken long, through phone calls and fax messages for them to develop a very close working relationship.

The fact that Sophia was a traffic-stopping beauty was secondary, but Mike had to admit, he enjoyed looking at her.

Yet could he trust a woman who plotted to marry her boss for his money? What should he do about it?

Teach her a lesson.

The notion rose in his mind and seemed brilliant in its conception. Yes. Sophia deserved to have the proverbial tables turned on her. She needed to see what it was like to be the victim of a carefully orchestrated seduction.

And he was just the man to do it.

Could he make Sophia fall for him? Could he get her to see beyond financial trappings to the man beneath the exterior? It was the only way to know for sure if Sophia was a hard-hearted mercenary without a conscience, or if given the opportunity to see the error of her thinking, would she indeed eschew money and follow her heart? It was the only way to know if something more lay beyond the physical attraction he felt for her. Michael had been burned before. He wasn't going to become emotionally invested in a woman until he knew for sure she loved him for himself and not for the Barrington name. Could he make her fall in love with Mike the mailman?

The idea excited him.

While Sophia was scheming to make Michael Barrington III fall in love with her, he was going to be doing a little scheming of his own.

Smiling, Mike pushed back his chair and got to his feet. He had a goal; all he needed was to put his plan into action.

No time like the present.

Sophia left the office at five-thirty, carrying a satchel filled with paperwork. Most everyone else had already gone for the day. Sophia frequently worked after hours to complete projects for Mr. Barrington and today was no exception. But she didn't mind. She wanted to prove to her boss she was a hard worker. Someone he could always rely on. Someone who would be there for him through thick and thin. Someone he could trust with his life.

She left the building through the side entrance, walking past the masonry wall flush with climbing bougainvillea and surrounded by oleander hedges. The relentless August heat followed her through the parking lot, beading sweat on her brow. Removing the scarf from around her neck, she blotted her forehead with it and entertained thoughts of a large soft drink poured over crushed ice.

Keys clutched in her right hand, she quickly opened the car door. The seat was excessively warm, despite the cardboard guard she'd placed in the window to protect the dashboard from the sun. She should have parked facing east not west.

"Ouch, ouch, ouch," she cried when she touched the key to the ignition and the hot metal burned her fingers. One of these days she was going to move to a cooler climate. She would already have left Arizona if it hadn't been for her mother.

Opening the vinyl console located between the driver's seat and the passenger side, Sophia removed a paper napkin and wrapped it around her hand to protect her skin while she tried the ignition again.

She heard an ominous click and nothing else.

No! Not more car problems.

Sighing, she rested her head against the steering wheel. In the last three weeks she'd had to buy a set of tires, a battery and two headlights. The vehicle was twelve years old with over a hundred and fifty thousand road miles and held together by little more than her prayers. Between living expenses and her mother's ongoing medical bills, Sophia existed from paycheck to paycheck. She couldn't afford for something else to be wrong with the car.

Taking a deep breath, she blotted her brow again before keying the ignition once more.

Same results.

What was she going to do now? Sophia moistened her lip with her tongue. She didn't have money for a taxi.

If only she had left work on time, she could have hitched a ride with a co-worker.

What to do?

One thing was for certain, she couldn't stay here in the roasting car. Sophia opened the door and got out, scanning the asphalt parking lot for a vehicle belonging to someone she knew. Surely she wasn't the only one working late.

At the far end of the lot there was a blue van parked next to a compact foreign car and beside that was...

A Harley-Davidson motorcycle.

With a man standing beside it, donning a helmet. Oh, no. Please not Mike.

Sophia gripped the car keys tighter. She'd rather spend the night in her office than ask *him* for a ride.

Mike straddled his Harley and revved the powerful engine.

Had he seen her? If he hadn't already, he would soon.

There was no leaving the parking lot without driving past her disabled vehicle.

Mother was home. Alone. And although Jannette Shepherd did all right throughout the day, she needed help getting to bed at night. Sophia couldn't stay at the office.

Pride goeth before a fall, Sophia thought grimly and shouldered her purse.

Mike spotted her standing there with her thumb stuck out like a hitchhiker. He pulled to a stop, raised the visor on his helmet and grinned at her.

"Going my way?" he asked.

"I need a ride," Sophia said. "My car's dead."

"That's a shame." He shook his head.

"I'll call a tow truck from home. If you can just give me a lift, I'd be eternally grateful."

"How grateful?" His grinned widened.

"Grateful enough to buy you dinner."

"Is that all?"

His joking irritated her. "Oh, forget it," she snapped. "I'll take my chances walking."

"I was just teasing, Sophia. Relax. You'd fry to a crisp before you could walk a mile. I'd be more than happy to give you a ride. Where do you live?"

"Sand Mesa Heights."

His eyebrow lifted. Obviously he knew the area. "That's a long way off," he replied, thankfully not pointing out it was also located in an older part of southern Phoenix that lately had been plagued by gang violence as the neighborhood had fallen into ruins. That was another reason she couldn't let her mother stay by herself at night.

"I've lived there all my life," Sophia said defensively, jutting out her chin, daring him to make a negative comment. She couldn't help where she came from.

"You'll need a helmet," Mike said mildly. "I keep an extra one in the mail room."

"What for?"

"Never can tell when you might find a lovely lady look-ing for a ride." He winked and Sophia wondered exactly how many women had ridden double with him on the Har-ley.

"Wanna come in with me?" He grinned, and a shiver of response raced up her spine.

"I'll wait here," she replied, not trusting herself to be alone with him in an empty building.

"Be back in a flash," he assured her.

Sophia waited while Mike trotted back into the Barring-ton building. She shouldn't be so excited, and yet she was. She realized she *wanted* to ride behind him, to feel the vibrating strum of that big motorcycle engine between her legs.

She watched Mike ascend the stairs as Rex Barrington came down them. Mr. Barrington was a kind, fatherly sort of man with excessive pride in the company he'd built from the ground up. He and Mike stopped on the steps and exchanged pleasantries. Mike pointed in her direction. Mr. Barrington waved. Sophia wriggled her fingers.

This is your opportunity. Flag down Mr. Barrington and ask him to take you home. He owns a Mercedes.

Nice as Mr. Barrington was, the man sort of intimidated Sophia with his keen intelligent green eyes. But, if she rode with him, she could ask him about Michael. Then again, she'd miss the chance to hang on to Mike's slim waist.

Torn, Sophia hesitated. In that minute, she saw a black Mercedes drive up to the curb and pick up Mr. Barrington, his secretary, Mildred Van Hess at the wheel.

Never mind, Sophia thought. She didn't want to intrude on what appeared to be more than an employer-employee relationship between the two of them.

Mike returned as quickly as he promised. He passed the

helmet to Sophia and swung aboard the motorcycle while she snapped it on and fastened the strap under her chin.

"What now?" she asked.

"Climb on behind me."

Sophia looked down at her short narrow skirt and back at Mike. "Yeah, right."

"Hike it up," he said.

Sucking in her breath, she did as he suggested, pulling the skirt up her thighs. His gaze blatantly traveled the length of her legs and he whistled low and long.

"Cut it out," Sophia huffed, grateful that the darkened visor hid her blush.

He laughed, loud and clear. "Get on, Miss Prim."

She swung a leg over the smooth warm leather. It molded like butter against her bare skin. She wrapped her arms around Mike's waist, but kept her hands clasped loosely in front of him.

He put the Harley in gear and the motorcycle shot forward. Sophia squealed her dismay and tightened her grip, clinging to him like a nettle to a cotton sock. He laughed again.

Sophia leaned up close enough to growl in his ear. "You did that on purpose."

Mike shrugged. It was admission enough of his guilt. "Hang on," he shouted and let out the throttle.

They weaved through late-afternoon traffic, the asphalt flying away beneath the tires. Sophia had never ridden a motorcycle before and she was terrified. The way Mike zigzagged through the cars had her heart leaping into her throat every few blocks.

But despite her fear, she experienced another sensation. One that took her by surprise. She felt exhilarated, liberated, freed. The palm trees and telephone poles flashed by on the arid roadside. The wind rushed over her skin raising goose bumps of pleasure. The pulsing engine beneath her legs felt like a live thing, sending a liquid heat throbbing through her bottom and up her spine. Her hands, laced together in front of Mike, could make out every muscle of his washboard-tight abdomen.

For the next twenty minutes, Sophia did nothing but feel. She didn't try to think or rationalize. She let her emotions flow in a jumble, slipping over her, around her, through her. At last she understood the appeal of a Harley. They were sexy machines, fast and strong, but plush and roomy, built for taking off, cruising the highway, leaving your troubles behind. They stirred the untamed wildness that lingered, if only a tiny bit, in almost everyone.

Mike shifted in his seat and prayed that Sophia wouldn't accidentally let her hands slip downward. If she did, she'd realize just how aroused he was. Her bare thighs were pressed hard on either side of his legs, and every time he turned his head left or right, he was assaulted by the sight of them. Slender, firm, richly flesh colored. And those shoes! Yikes! Crimson in color with three-inch heels.

Her breasts, resting against the back of his chest were almost as much of a distraction as those delicious legs. The blouse she wore was soft and silky, making it feel as if there wasn't much between Sophia's bare skin and him.

Maybe disabling her car and offering her a ride on the Hog hadn't been such a bright idea after all. He hadn't expected to feel so out of control by a little physical contact.

"Which way?" Mike asked when they came to a stop at an intersection. He let the engine idle at the red light, his feet planted firmly on the ground to balance them.

This part of Phoenix was older than the area of town where the Barrington Corporation was housed. Mike rarely ventured out this way. Many of the storefronts were vacant. Graffiti defaced bus benches and the sides of buildings. Litter lined the gutters and glass beer bottles were nestled against overflowing trash cans. Clumps of young men in tank tops and tattoos stood on the street corner, eyeing the Harley and Sophia covetously. An uneasy feeling settled over Mike. Sophia lived in this neighborhood?

"Take a right," Sophia directed. "Go six blocks and make another right. You'll come to Santa Teresa Drive. Take a left at the second stop sign. That's Red Rock Circle. It dead-ends at my driveway."

He followed her instructions, cruising down the narrow streets. The smell of numerous suppers being prepared filled the air. He caught a whiff of chili powder and jalapeños. Most of the residences were small and old, with peeling paint jobs and untended lawns.

At one house on Santa Teresa Drive a group of children in dirty T-shirts played on the sidewalk while an elderly woman with a worn expression sat motionless in a rocking chair, keeping watch from the wide screened-in porch. Sophia waved her hand in greeting. Wary at first because they didn't recognize her on the back of the Harley, the children hesitated before raising their hands in response.

"Señorita Sophia," they called after her in greeting, "where did you get the motorcycle?"

"It belongs to my friend, Mike," she called back.

My friend.

It felt good to hear her say that. Except Mike wanted to be much more than Sophia's friend.

The house where he stopped on Red Rock Circle wasn't in any better condition than the rest, except here, a flower garden flourished. Mike wasn't good at naming flowers, but they were pretty ones in many shades and hues and emitted a deliciously fragrant aroma that welcomed him like a hug. A large white cat lay curled beneath a birdbath under an olive tree and this was where Sophia ran the minute Mike shut off the engine.

"Shu-Shu," she greeted, peeling off the helmet and letting it slide to the ground before scooping the cat into her arms.

Watching her cuddle the animal to her cheek caused something warm and slippery to break away in Mike's heart.

In an instant, Sophia's persona shifted. She was no longer the professional working woman, assistant to the vice president of the Barrington Corporation. Gone was the efficient secretary he knew and in her place stood a happy little girl.

Mike swallowed. Hard. What was happening? He was supposed to be making Sophia fall in love with him. Not the other way around.

She turned to smile. "Thanks for the ride home, Mike. It was sweet of you."

Sweet, hell. He was the one who'd taken the starter off her car. "It was nothing."

"I believe I owe you dinner." She raised her head and sniffed the air. "And unless I miss my guess, Mother's made her fabulous arroz con polo tonight."

"Perhaps I should be going," he said, feeling like a giant heel for messing with her car. He was determined to get back and fix it before going home.

"I know she's got strawberry cheesecake for dessert," Sophia tempted. "It's my favorite and she made it for my birthday. That's why I had a light lunch. I wanted to save my calories for the cheesecake."

As if she had any trouble watching her figure. Mike trailed his gaze over her firm slender form.

"I'm sure your mother wasn't expecting company for supper."

Sophia waved her hand. "She always makes too much. Come, come." Still holding Shu-Shu the cat, she motioned him up the stoop.

The ease with which Sophia invited him in, trusting that his motives were honorable, increased Mike's shame.

Remember, he reminded himself, *you're just out to teach her a valuable lesson about integrity.*

"Mother," she called, pushing open the screen door into the house that was almost as warm inside as it was out. All the windows were open and numerous floor fans hummed noisily. The smell of rice and chicken made Mike's mouth water.

"In the kitchen, honey. You're late."

"I know." Sophia kicked off her high heels in the corner.

The living room was small and overstuffed with cheap knickknacks but spotlessly clean. The furniture was old and faded by the sun streaming in through the windows. Guilt twisted Mike's gut. He had no idea Sophia came from such humble surroundings. It went a long way in explaining her determination to marry a rich man.

He made a mental note to give her a raise. A substantial one. She deserved one and besides, if Sophia had enough money of her own, perhaps she wouldn't feel such a need to have a man provide for her.

Sophia led the way to the kitchen, still talking as she went. Feeling out of place, Mike followed reluctantly.

"The car broke down," Sophia said to her mother. "I had to get a ride home with a co-worker, and I asked him to stay for dinner."

"The car?" Sophia's mother sounded alarmed. "Not again!"

Another twist of the guilt knife. Mike winced.

"Mother," Sophia said, placing a hand on Mike's shoulder and ushering him into the kitchen, "this is Mike."

Mike paused in the doorway. Sophia's mother was

seated in a wheelchair, stirring a pot on a stove that had been made lower than normal. It startled him to realize that Sophia's mother was confined to a wheelchair. He'd had no idea.

She was a thin woman with blond hair now streaked with silver and eyes as blue as Sophia's. And even in her mid-forties she was still an attractive woman. But there was a hardness in her eyes that wasn't in her daughter's. A rough edge that said life had kicked her around one time too many.

"Michael." She smiled and extended her hand. "So nice to meet you at last. My name's Jannette."

"He's not Michael Barrington, Mother," Sophia said. "He's Mike from the mail room."

Mike had the feeling that mother and daughter had discussed Michael Barrington on more than one occasion. He began to wonder if Jannette Shepherd was behind Sophia's desire to marry her boss. If that were true, all the more reason to coax Sophia into falling in love with him. He owed it to her. In a sense, he'd be liberating her from her mother's control. Sophia needed to make her own mistakes.

"Oh." Instantly the welcoming expression on Jannette's face was eclipsed by disappointment, but she quickly hid it from him. "Well, Mike, thank you for bringing Sophia home. You are planning on staying for dinner with us, aren't you?"

"If you're sure you've got enough."

"Absolutely," Jannette replied. "Sophia, honey, why don't you set the table?"

The food was delicious. Mike had no quibble with Jannette's cooking abilities but he couldn't shake the feeling that she didn't approve of him. He glanced up a time or two to find her studying him with displeasure. In attempt to make peace with her, he smiled often and boyishly. Generally his grin worked like a charm with women, but it only seemed to agitate Sophia's mother.

"So Mike," Jannette said at last. "How long have you been working in the mail room?"

Aha, he thought. Now we get down to the nitty-gritty. The mailman isn't good enough for her daughter.

"A few months," he replied.

"Where did you work before coming to the Barrington Corporation?" Jannette asked.

"Here and there."

"I see. How old are you, Mike? Thirty-two?"

"Thirty-six."

"And you still work in the mail room?"

"Mother," Sophia said, clearly scandalized. "Mike and I aren't dating. He just gave me a ride home."

Jannette smiled an apology. "I'm sorry to put you on the spot, Mike, but you must understand. I'm a single mother and Sophia is my only child. I want the best for her."

"I understand, Mrs. Shepherd."

And he did. The modest house, the meager surroundings, the wheelchair. He didn't know the whole story but her motives were easy enough to figure. Jannette wanted a way out of poverty for her daughter. In her eyes, marrying a rich man was the ticket.

"Thank you for the meal," he said after they had eaten the cheesecake and sang happy birthday to a blushing Sophia. He noticed she didn't tell her mother about the glass cat paperweight he had given her. "The food was delicious."

"Thank you for seeing Sophia home safe and sound."

"I'll have a look at her car," he said, his eyes boldly

meeting Jannette's. "I'm pretty good at fixing things. Maybe I can save you some money."

"That's very considerate of you, Mike. We appreciate it." Jannette never dropped her gaze. Even though her voice was pleasant, her underlying message wasn't hard to decipher: *"stay away from my daughter."*

"I'd better be going," Mike said.

"I'll walk you outside." Sophia got up to follow him.

Twilight had gathered while they were inside having supper. Overhead, a few bright early stars shone down. Shu-Shu, purring happily, eeled between Sophia's legs. Sophia reached into her pocket and gave him her car keys.

"I'll pick you up tomorrow morning," he said. "About seven-fifteen?"

"All right."

"The food was good. Thanks for dinner."

"I want to apologize for my mother," Sophia said. "She's had a hard life."

"Nothing to apologize for," Mike replied, picking up his helmet and straddling the motorcycle.

"She means well."

"I understand. Only the best for her daughter. And that excludes mailmen."

"Mike, I..."

Light from the street lamp shone down on her in a hazy glow. She looked so damned beautiful standing there that his heart caught in his throat and his head reeled dizzily.

Mike had no inkling what was coming next. Sophia took him completely by surprise.

She leaned over the handlebars of the Harley, favoring him with an unbelievable view of her cleavage. While his eyes were transfixed by her exquisite flesh, she gently cupped his chin in her palm and kissed him on the mouth.

Lightly, quickly, like a butterfly kissing a flower.

He hissed in air.

Without another word, Sophia turned and fled into the house, shutting the door closed solidly behind her and leaving Mike wondering what in the heck had just happened between them.

Chapter Three

"Stay away from that boy," Jannette warned. "He's bad news in the making."

"He's not a boy," Sophia replied, standing before the bathroom mirror and combing out her damp curls from her shower.

Her mother sat in the doorway, a frown on her face. Sophia lightly traced her fingers over her lips, which still vibrated from brushing gently against Mike's mouth. Her spontaneous kiss had surprised her as much as him. The lingering effects had surprised her even more.

"That's exactly why you should stay away from him. A thirty-six-year-old man who still works in the mail room and rides a motorcycle is nothing but trouble with a capital *T*."

"Mother," Sophia chided, studying her face in the mirror for any signs of wrinkles. "I'm not getting any younger."

"So now you're willing to settle for anything?"

Sophia sighed. "Mike's just a friend."

"Friends can easily turn into lovers."

"He is cute, isn't he?" Sophia said, more to irritate her mother than anything else.

For the last twenty-nine years her mother had dictated every detail of her life by telling her whom not to date and whom to pursue, and Sophia was growing tired of it. If it hadn't been for her mother's illness, Sophia would have clipped the proverbial apron strings long ago. It was way past time for a little rebellion.

"Yes, he is handsome," Jannette said sharply. "There's nothing more dangerous than a handsome man. They'll lie to you, rob you of your hopes and dreams, then discard you like yesterday's dust."

"Every man isn't like my father," Sophia said softly.

"Sophia, you've got to think about your future and the future of any children you may have. I only want what's best for you. Please, honey, try to understand. I'm begging you, don't repeat my mistakes. Promise me you won't see Mike again."

"He's giving me a ride to work tomorrow."

"You know what I mean."

"Calm down, I'm not 'seeing' him. We work in the same building. That's all."

"I thought you liked your boss," Jannette said. "What happened with that?"

"I do like him."

"But..."

"There are no buts. Mr. Barrington is a very kind, hard-working man."

"And he's overseas while Mike is here."

"Yes," Sophia admitted.

Jannette shook her head. "This isn't good. Can't you do something to convince your boss to come home sooner than planned? The next time you speak to him could you let it slip that his father is really ready to retire?"

"Mother." Sophia sighed her exasperation.

"Well, can you?"

"I wouldn't mislead Mr. Barrington just to get him to come home to Phoenix."

"You don't have to lie, honey. Tell him his father is anxious to start his new life. That's true, isn't it?"

"It's not that simple. So what if Michael comes home? That doesn't mean he'll fall in love with me."

Her mother maneuvered the wheelchair closer and gently stroked Sophia's arm. "Who wouldn't fall in love with you? You're beautiful and talented. You've got a gorgeous figure. You're smart and hardworking. You'd make a splendid wife for any man. Michael will recognize that about you instantly."

Sophia shook her head and expressed her concerns aloud. "Isn't it sort of underhanded, plotting to marry someone? I mean you've always taught me how important it is to be honest in your relationships."

Her mother laughed. "If you don't plot, then you'll get shafted like I did. I wasn't smart enough, but women have been snaring men with their feminine wiles for years. That's how things are. Don't discard everything you've ever dreamed of over some good-looking guy with bad intentions. Don't throw away all those etiquette lessons I worked two jobs to pay for. Please don't sell yourself short. You're special, Sophia. You know how to act like a rich man's wife, and that's what you'll be if you listen to your mother."

But Jannette's promise sounded hollow to Sophia and more than a little sad. She stared at her mother in the mirror, felt Jannette's fingers curl tightly around the sleeve of her bathrobe.

Her mother was frightened, Sophia realized suddenly. Terrified that she would run off with Mike the mailman on his Harley and leave her alone to fend for herself. Her heart ached at the desperation etched on Jannette's face.

"Don't worry, Mother, taking care of you is always my first priority," she said.

"Who said anything about me? I had my shot and I blew it. I just don't want you to hurt your chance at happiness."

"I promise, I won't do anything stupid."

Jannette's relief was palpable. "Mark my word, Sophia. When Mr. Barrington shows up to sweep you off your feet, you'll feel like Cinderella at the ball."

Yeah, Sophia thought glumly, but what happens at the stroke of midnight?

Mike arrived on her doorstep at seven-fifteen sharp, with her car instead of his motorcycle parked in the driveway.

"You fixed my car," she exclaimed, running her gaze over him and trying her best not to notice how sexy he looked in blue jeans. Mike wore a short-sleeved chambray shirt and new running shoes. It was Friday and the Barrington Corporation allowed for casual dress on the last day of the work week.

Sophia herself wore a white peasant blouse embroidered with pink and blue flowers, and pale blue slacks. Her cloth belt and low-heeled shoes were a matching pink. She had her hair caught back in a ponytail wrapped with pink and blue ribbon. She'd dressed for a motorcycle ride to work. As happy as she was to see her car in good working order, she couldn't help feeling a little regretful that she wasn't going to get another trip on the Harley.

"What was wrong with it?" she asked, stepping off the porch and crossing the driveway to her car.

"The starter."

"How much do I owe you?" she asked, opening her purse.

"Don't worry about it." Mike waved away the bills Sophia flashed at him.

"But I insist. You've been so nice."

"Please," he said. "I can't take money from you."

The tone of his voice caught her attention. She looked over to see something akin to guilt in his eyes and was confused by what she saw. What did Mike have to feel guilty about?

"I may be poor but I'm proud." Sophia moved to thrust the cash into his shirt pocket.

"Dammit, Sophia, I said no." He grabbed her wrist.

His touch seared her. Startled, she looked into his green eyes. *Don't push it!* his gaze declared.

"Come on, Mike, I know the mail room doesn't pay a lot. I make more money than you do."

"I don't need a lot of money," he said gruffly, letting go of her arm. "That fabulous meal your mother cooked last night was payment enough. If you feel you must do more, then you can give me a ride home from work this afternoon."

"Fair enough," she replied, stuffing the money back in her purse. "Get in."

He climbed into the passenger side and Sophia slid beneath the wheel. The car started without a hitch.

"How's your mother this morning?" Mike asked after a few minutes had passed.

"She's fine."

"Jannette doesn't like me much." He said it as a statement of fact, not a question.

"It's nothing personal. She's very protective of me. I'm all she's got."

"She seemed to like me when she thought I was 'the Third,'" Mike observed.

"What can I say?" Sophia shrugged. "My mother is impressed by money."

"Like mother, like daughter?"

"Excuse me?" Sophia flashed Mike an angry stare as she drove from Sand Mesa Heights and onto the freeway. Traffic was thick and demanded her concentration.

"Forget it," Mike mumbled.

"No, go ahead," Sophia said, switching on her turn signal. "Get it off your chest."

He raised his hands. "It's none of my business."

"You're darned right it's not."

"But you shouldn't let hard times drive you into doing something stupid like marrying a man you're not in love with just so you can be taken care of financially."

Sophia glared and honked her horn at a red convertible that cut her off. "Who says I don't love Michael."

"Oh, come on, Sophia. Give me a break. You can't love someone you've never even met."

"That's not true. People fall in love over the Internet, and haven't you heard about people who fall in love with a photograph of someone? It happens."

"Where does it happen?" he taunted.

"In that movie *Laura*, where Dana Andrews falls in love with a portrait of Gene Tierney."

"That's a movie, Sophia."

"Still, it could happen."

Mike snorted. "You don't even know what the man looks like. He could be the Hunchback of Notre Dame for all you know."

"I doubt that. Rex Barrington is a handsome man."

"Genetics are no guarantee that Michael isn't ugly."

"Jealous?"

"Me?" Mike looked amused. "What do I have to be jealous about?"

"Michael's physical appearance doesn't matter to me."

"That's right," Mike said almost inaudibly. "It's his money that attracts you. You know it's got to be hard being Michael Barrington, never knowing for sure if a woman likes you for yourself or for what you can buy her. I don't envy the man.''

''I'm sure you don't,'' Sophia snapped. ''Michael works hard for what he's got.''

''Oh, yeah. It must be real hard inheriting money.''

''What's your problem?''

''Gold diggers turn my stomach.''

''Are you accusing me of being a gold digger?'' Sophia pulled over on the shoulder of the freeway and stomped solidly on the brake. She slammed the car into Park and turned in her seat to shoot daggers at Mike with her eyes.

''If the shoe fits...''

''You think you know everything, don't you?'' She flung the words at him. ''Well, you don't.''

''I know your mother's pushing you to marry a rich man.''

''So what if she is?'' Sophia shouted. ''Is it so wrong to want the best for your child?''

''Is a loveless marriage a good thing?''

''It's as easy to fall in love with a rich man as a poor one,'' she retorted tartly.

''What happened to your father?'' he asked. ''Why isn't he in the picture?''

''That—'' she pointed angrily at him with her index finger ''—is none of your business, mister.''

''What's the problem? Wasn't he rich enough to suit the Shepherd women?''

''You don't know what you're talking about!''

''You're twenty-nine years old and letting your mother run your life. Telling you who's worthy of your love and who's not.''

''I ought to make you walk,'' she threatened.

''Yeah?'' He leaned across the seat to glare back at her. ''Yeah.''

His green eyes were quicksand, his rapid breathing heated carbon against her skin.

Chemistry.

Hot, messy, explosive.

It slammed into Sophia with the momentum of a lab experiment gone horribly awry.

Except this wasn't a lab and being this close to such a sexy volatile man in morning rush-hour traffic wasn't an experiment she recommended even to the bravest souls.

Before she knew what was happening, Mike was kissing her. Right there on Highway 10.

Hungrily, greedily, he cupped the back of her head in one palm and drew her across the car toward him.

Her seat belt was in the way. Sophia clawed it off, desperate to get to Mike. He was jerking at his restraint, as well.

His lips sank down on hers. Smothering her in a deliciously warm wetness. Stealing her breath, stealing her mind, stealing her senses until she was deaf, dumb and blind with desire for him.

Sophia kissed him back, as hard and fierce as he kissed her. She fought a mad urge to rip off her blouse and bare her breasts to him. She wanted him here, now, this minute with a passion that terrified her in its intensity.

He smelled so good. Tasted even better. She couldn't get enough, would never get enough of him.

Their attraction was not a fluke, not some freak twist of nature, not an aberrant occurrence. This was real and very, very scary.

Mike's quicksilver tongue prodded, demanding entry into her mouth. Sophia parted her lips and eagerly let him in.

Her fingers gripped his well-knit shoulder muscles. She closed her eyes and fell down, down, down into an endless sea of ravenous physical cravings.

Lust.

Unadulterated. Raw. Compelling.

Feelings, sensations, intense emotions that Sophia had never before experienced swelled over her like a violent hurricane devouring a small tropical island, scattering everything into the wind, destroying everything in its wake.

So this was what her mother had been warning her against these many years. At last Sophia understood. This helplessness in the face of physical urges. This headlong wantonness of her body aching to merge with his. This mindless desire that begged her to ignore all sense and reason for the sake of ultimate satisfaction.

A momentary satisfaction that could possibly create an unwanted child.

Sophia whimpered.

Mike swallowed her whimper with his greedy mouth.

But this could not, must not happen. How could it anyway, in this small vehicle, on the side of the road, sun flooding in through the windows, cars honking encouragement as they drove past, the smell of tar and fuel exhaust clogging the air?

Brought back to reality, Sophia stopped kissing him.

As if perfectly in tune with her, Mike pulled back and sucked in an unsteady breath.

''Wow,'' he whispered softly. ''Wow.''

Shakily Sophia drew a finger across her mouth. She forced herself to focus on the steering wheel. She straightened her blouse which had gotten twisted. She raked her fingers through her hair. She slipped her safety belt back on. Her hands trembled as she put the car into gear, pressed on the accelerator and entered the stream of traffic. Not once did she dare look over at him.

Mike uttered not another sound on the remainder of the way into the office.

* * *

Wow. Wow. Wow.

Mike could not stop thinking about her. In all his thirty-six years he had never been so captivated by any woman. Sophia had been running through his head all morning, searing a beaten path across his brain. In a daze, he wandered through the building delivering mail. Those few stunning moments in Sophia's car had stolen his free will. So clouded were his senses, he could barely drag one foot in front of the other, much less return the hearty greetings of his co-workers.

His mind was clouded with visions of her and nothing else. Sophia. Blond, beautiful, a lusty princess hiding behind a carefully constructed facade. Sophia. The perfect secretary, hardworking, devoted, efficient. Sophia. So full of fire, so full of passion. Her anger had lit the wick of their simmering desire, sending it flaming into a raging maelstrom of physical delight.

How had he lived for so long without this heady feeling? How had he existed for so long without her?

Don't lose your sense of direction, he scolded himself. *You didn't get where you are today by falling for every pretty face that sent your temperature soaring.*

Except no woman had ever made him feel the way Sophia did. Whenever he was around her, he felt stronger, smarter, brighter. Something about her made him feel more of a man. Mike found himself aching to tell her all his secrets, to reveal every silly daydream that had ever sprinted through his head, to bore her with stories of his childhood, to regale her with his jokes. To reveal to her his true identity.

Watch out!

He could never forget that Sophia, sexy as she might be, could not be trusted. At least not yet. Not until she passed his litmus test of falling in love with Mike the mail-man.

What if he couldn't change her? What if he turned on the charm, courted her with a heretofore undemonstrated fervency but to no avail? What if he pulled out all the stops and despite his best efforts, she still chose Michael Barrington over him? Then he'd be left with egg on his face and his heart in his hands.

Did he dare take that risk?

Mike suppressed a laugh. How ironic, the master of risk-taking reduced to a quivering mass by a mere woman.

Too bad she didn't have more money of her own. If Sophia had a substantial raise in pay and more job security maybe then she'd stop viewing men as a meal ticket. Maybe then she'd develop confidence in her own abilities to generate an income and she'd be free to follow her heart.

It wasn't as if she didn't need the money. Mike had seen how she lived and he felt the pain of her poverty. He must see that she got a raise.

"Hey, Mike." Jack Cavanaugh greeted him enthusiastically when Mike pushed through the door and into the spacious rooms of the advertising department.

"Morning, Jack."

Jack's smile was wider than usual. "Did you catch the baseball game last night? Phoenix trounced the Wild Cats."

Mike shook his head.

"Too busy, huh?" Jack winked.

"Busy?" Mike repeated the word, struggling to pay attention to his friend. Before Jack had started dating his assistant, Molly Doyle, he and Mike had gone to a minor league baseball game at least once a week. Now Jack took Molly instead.

He missed Jack, Mike realized. Before coming to work

as the mailman at the Barrington Corporation, Mike had never really had any close friendships. Even as a boy he'd been hesitant to let down his guard and make friends. Too many moves from city to city, school to school, as his father built his empire. Too many false friends. Too many bad experiences had taught him to be cautious. Mike was always on the alert, wary of kids who only wanted to be with him for his father's money. Throughout most of his childhood he'd felt like he was on the outside looking in, never really quite sure what others thought about him.

It hadn't helped that Rex had always been too busy to play catch or to take him to baseball games. He was supposed to understand. Making money came before time spent with the family. It was a fact of the Barrington household he'd learned to live with. A fact that had taught him never to depend on anyone.

He had courted this persona, taking pride in his independence, knowing he didn't need others for his self-esteem. It had spurred the rebellious phase he'd gone through in his late teens, when in the aftermath of his mother's illness, he and Rex had not gotten along. Michael's occasional feelings of isolation had intensified upon his mother's death, and he supposed that was part of what motivated him to hold himself at a distance in his personal relationships. This deep-seated fear of getting too involved, of being betrayed again. It was a fear of losing something important. A fear that directly conflicted with his sudden need to win Sophia's love.

Perhaps it would be wiser if he stopped things right here and did not pursue Sophia any further. The same prudence that guided him in making deals, urged him to drop his plot to make her fall in love with the mailman and keep his heart safe.

"Don't play innocent with me, you sly dog." Jack came around his desk to slap Mike on the shoulder. "Nick Delaney saw you yesterday evening with Sophia Shepherd on the back of your Harley.''

''I was just giving Sophia a ride home.''

Jack winked again. ''Right. And that's why Sam Wainwright spotted you getting out of Sophia's car this morning.'' Jack raised his palms. ''Hey, it's nothing to be ashamed of. Sophia's a very pretty girl.''

Inwardly Mike groaned. None of his plans had included exposing Sophia to office gossip.

''But you better be careful.'' Jack glanced around the office to see if anyone else was in hearing distance. He lowered his voice. ''There's a rumor that Sophia belongs to 'the Third.' ''

''Oh, yeah?''

Jack nodded. ''I heard it from Molly who heard it from Olivia Hunter.''

Mike scowled. ''I'm surprised at you, Jack, spreading unfounded gossip.''

''Hey, I'm only looking to protect you. If Sophia's in tight with the boss, I wouldn't want you to lose your job over her.''

''She is not in tight with the boss,'' Mike snapped, irritated by his friend. He knew Jack didn't really mean anything by the innuendo, and normally such a minor thing wouldn't have gotten to him. But by gosh, he didn't want the entire office believing that Sophia and Michael Barrington were an item when he knew for a fact the rumor was nothing more than Sophia's wishful thinking.

Jack sobered. ''You really like her, don't you?''

''She's nice enough.''

''Come on, buddy, you can't fool me. I wore the same silly grin on my face when I started getting serious about Molly.''

''Sophia's not interested in me.'' Mike shook his head.

''How do you know?''

"I just know," Mike said, wishing he hadn't gotten into this discussion with Jack. "Here's your mail." He passed him a stack of colorful glossy envelopes.

"Thanks."

Mike left the advertising department with nagging doubts following him. What to do about Sophia? Things were trickier than Jack would ever know.

In fact, there was only one person who would completely understand his situation. Only one man could give him the proper perspective. And he sorely needed that advice before he made the wrong move and ruined everything.

Getting off the elevator on the fifth floor, Mike walked past Mildred Van Hess's desk. The impeccably dressed executive secretary glanced up at his approach.

"Hey, Mildred." He smiled. Mildred was the only employee at the Barrington Corporation who knew he was masquerading as Mike the mailman.

She smiled back. "Good morning, Michael."

"The big guy in?"

Mildred nodded.

"Is he busy?"

"Never too busy to talk to you."

"That's good," Mike said. "Because I'm packing one heck of a problem."

He darted a quick glance in the direction of Sophia's office and was relieved to see that her door was closed. Taking a deep breath, he squared his shoulders and entered Rex Barrington's plush suite.

"Hi, Dad," he said to the distinguished man sitting behind the large marble desk, his reading glasses perched on the end of his nose.

"Morning, son."

Mike prowled restlessly around the room, his hands clasped behind his back. He stared out the big picture windows at the traffic below. In the distance, he could see the desert.

Rex put down his paperwork. "How are things going?"

"I don't know," Michael said honestly. "I'm worried about Sophia Shepherd."

"What do you mean?"

"I'm not sure I can trust her."

Rex lifted his eyebrows in surprise. "Sophia seems like a very sweet girl to me and Mildred tells me she's an excellent secretary."

"She is," Michael said, perching on the arm of a leather chair and running his hands through his hair.

"I'm listening."

"I'm afraid she's another Erica."

The sound of that ugly name from the past ended the conversation momentarily.

"Are you sure?" Rex frowned. "I'd hate to believe something like that about her."

"It's worse than that," Michael assured his father.

"Oh?"

"I think I might be falling in love with her."

Chapter Four

Sophia was confused. So confused that so far that morning she had already put salt in her coffee, accidentally deleted some important e-mail that had to be reentered and overwatered the ficus tree in the office to the point of saturating the carpet beneath it.

Damn Mike! This was all his doing. Sophia, on her hands and knees, sopped up water from the carpet with a roll of heavyweight paper towels and tried her best not to cry.

How on earth could she be so attracted to him when what she really wanted was to marry Michael Barrington?

Or did she?

It hadn't been Michael Barrington who'd given her a kiss so shocking it had scorched her socks.

But Michael was the man she respected. He could provide for a wife and family. He was considerate and thoughtful and hardworking. He had goals and dreams and ambitions.

Who got you a birthday gift and who didn't?

Well, she could hardly hold Michael responsible for that, could she? He was a busy man. Mike on the other hand, had time to spare. Michael wasn't even in the same country; he couldn't be held to the same expectations.

The phone rang.

Hurriedly Sophia got to her feet and dropped the soggy towels in the trash can. She dried her hands with a clean paper towel and snagged the receiver on the third jangle.

"Michael Barrington's office. Sophia Shepherd speaking."

The instant his rich voice washed over her, Sophia inhaled sharply.

"Good morning, Sophia," Michael Barrington greeted her, his tone teasing.

"Oh, Mr. Barrington. How are you this morning?" Her stomach fluttered and her heart contracted. Only one other person on the planet stirred her like this and he worked in the mail room.

"Sophia," he chided. "How many times have I told you that it's okay to call me Michael?"

"I know, sir," she said, "but since we haven't even met face-to-face, I don't want to be presumptuous."

"It would never be presumptuous for you to call me by my first name, and whatever you do, please get rid of the 'sir.' It makes me feel like my father."

"Yes, sir...er...Michael."

"That's better."

Lord, that voice! So firm, so commanding.

So similar to Mike the mailman.

That thought gave Sophia pause. Was Mike's voice the subliminal thing that attracted her to him? Could it be he reminded her of Michael Barrington and that was the explanation for her desire? She certainly hoped so! If that were indeed the case then she had no reason to feel guilty for her response to Mike's kisses in the car. In essence, she had been responding to Michael's voice.

But what about Mike's lips on hers? His hands in her hair. The smell and taste of him? How could she explain away those things?

"How's business this morning?" Michael asked, his voice wrapping around her, tight as a hug.

Sophia gave him a rundown on the business accounts while her mind whirled. She was caught! Trapped between two lovers. Well, not lovers exactly, but two men who were both becoming increasingly more important to her.

"Excellent work," Michael complimented.

A delicious warmth seeped through Sophia's body at his praise. "Just doing my job, sir."

"What?"

"Michael." She smiled into the receiver.

"Very good."

"Old habits die hard," she confessed.

"Listen, Sophia," he said, and she heard a hesitation in his voice. It wasn't like Michael to hesitate, and for that split second he sounded exactly like Mike the mailman.

"Yes?" She leaned forward against her desk, trying hard to fight the excitement pushing through her chest.

"It has come to my attention that I happened to have missed your birthday yesterday."

"Oh, I didn't expect you to remember my birthday." Sophia leaned back in her chair and ran a hand through her curls. "After all, we've only been working together a few months and you're a very busy man."

"Stop making excuses for me, Sophia. I forgot your birthday and that's inexcusable."

"Don't worry about it."

"I don't worry, I correct my oversights."

As if on cue, a knock sounded at her open door and a deliveryman appeared with a vivid display of flowers clutched in his arms. Dozens and dozens of them. Roses and lilies. Orchids and daisies. Carnations and gladiola. Red, green, purple, yellow, orange. A fragrant rainbow protruding from a leaded crystal vase.

"Flowers for Miss Sophia Shepherd," the deliveryman called out.

"Michael!" she breathed into the phone, and waved the man over to her desk. "What have you done?"

She heard his sexy chuckle. "I take it they've arrived."

"They're so beautiful!"

Sudden tears sprang to her eyes. Emotion choked her throat. She felt like a princess, showered with affection. How had she, for one second, thought the sexual passion she shared with Mike the mailman could possibly eclipse the deep-seated respect she held for Michael Barrington?

"And that's not all," Michael said, still speaking while Sophia groped for a tissue to dab at her eyes.

The deliveryman plunked the flowers in front of her and winked before leaving the room.

"It's n-not?" Sophia stammered, overwhelmed by Michael's generous gesture.

"No, ma'am. I'm giving you a raise. And it's not for your birthday, it's for all the hard work you do."

"Oh, that's not necessary. Really. I enjoy my job."

"Hush for a minute and listen." He named a figure so high, Sophia sputtered.

"What?" she said.

He repeated the amount of her raise.

"That's almost double my current salary!" Sophia exclaimed in disbelief. She could buy a new car and pay off some of Jannette's long-standing medical bills. "Surely you can't mean it."

"You're worth every penny and more."

"I...I don't know what to say." Fresh tears welled in her eyes. "Thank you, thank you, thank you."

"You're very welcome. I wouldn't want anyone trying to steal you away from me."

Steal you away.

She knew he was talking about work. Yes, she did. But guilt conjured up another image. The one of Mike kissing her heatedly in her car on the side of the freeway. She gulped.

"No one could ever steal me away from you," Sophia replied adamantly. She twisted the telephone cord around one finger and dreamily doodled, *Mrs. Rex Michael Barrington III,* on her desk calendar with the opposite hand.

"You never can tell when you might run across a smooth-talking headhunter full of glib promises. I need to know that you're loyal to the Barrington Corporation, Sophia."

"Oh, absolutely. I'm committed to this company."

"That's good to hear. I hope you enjoy the flowers, and happy birthday."

"Thanks again."

"We'll talk tomorrow."

"Until tomorrow."

"Wait," he said, before she had time to hang up. "There's something else I've been meaning to ask you."

"Yes?"

Silence hummed across the lines. Sophia could picture Michael at his office in Germany, handsome in an expensively tailored suit, the receiver cradled under his chin, his feet propped on his desk in the casual elegance of a self-assured monarch.

"Are you seeing anyone?"

"Beg your pardon?" The question caught her off guard. "What do you mean?"

"Do you have a boyfriend?"

Sophia caught her breath as a thrill sped through her. Could it be true? Was Michael asking her out? This was too much. A substantial raise in pay, a beautiful floral bouquet and an invitation to go out with Michael Barrington all in one day?

"No," she answered, and pinched herself.

"Are you sure there's not someone special in your life?"

Guiltily she thought of Mike. He was special. She couldn't deny the sparks that flew between them whenever they were in the same room together. But no matter how hot the chemistry, she had no future with Mike the mailman, and for the last four months, she'd dreamed constantly of the moment when Michael Barrington would ask her out on a date. And even though Sophia valued honesty above all things, she wasn't about to blow this opportunity by telling him about Mike.

"No," she spoke firmly, ignoring the twinge of remorse. Mike had made her no promises; she owed him nothing.

"I'm surprised," Michael said. "I'd have bet money that a woman with a voice as beautiful as yours would be fending the men off with a long-handled stick."

"There's no one," she assured him, resolutely pushing thoughts of Mike from her mind. It was true. She and Mike had never actually dated. They weren't an item. "Is there any particular reason you ask?" She braved the question, crossed her fingers and prayed.

"Well, I was just going to tell you to bring your boyfriend along to the company picnic in two weeks."

"Huh?" Sophia blinked. Had she heard right?

"I wanted to meet him, shake his hand and tell him how lucky he was to have such a reliable girlfriend."

Reliable? Sophia's chest tightened. She'd gotten it all wrong. Michael wasn't asking her out.

"But since you don't have a boyfriend, guess I'll just have to shake your hand instead."

Shake her hand? Well, that was a comedown to reality. Sophia swallowed back her disappointment.

"You'll be at the company picnic?"

"I'm going to do my best to wind things up here in Frankfurt by then," he said.

Hope sprang fresh and new in her heart. At last! She'd be able to meet the object of her long-held affections and put her plan into action. Once he got to know her in person, Sophia was certain Michael would ask her out.

"Until tomorrow."

"Goodbye," she whispered.

The phone clicked softly in her ear as Michael severed the connection, leaving Sophia feeling frustrated and more confused than ever.

From a desk across the hall, Michael Barrington cradled the receiver and glanced over at his father. Essentially, by sending Sophia flowers, he had upped the ante, pitting himself against himself. Michael against Mike. The wealthy man versus the charming bad boy. Who would emerge the victor?

"You sure this is the right thing to do?" he asked Rex.

"It's the only way you're going to know for sure if you can trust her, son. You know how important trust is in any relationship. If Sophia is to remain your assistant, you've got to know that she'll be loyal to you and the company no matter what."

Michael made a face. "I suppose you're right."

But he couldn't help feeling that misleading Sophia about his true identity was a very underhanded thing indeed.

"She lied," Michael said softly.

"Lied?" Rex tilted his head in the comforting manner he used when he wanted someone to open up to him. "About what?"

"She said there was no one special in her life."

"Perhaps there's not."

"Then what do you call Mike the mailman? Surely the woman doesn't go around kissing every man the way she kisses him." Michael folded his arms over his chest, realizing Sophia's denial of a love interest cut him deeper than he thought possible.

"Son." Rex placed a hand on his shoulder. "This is something you're going to have to work out on your own."

"I need your advice."

Nervously Sophia wrung her hands. It was two o'clock in the afternoon and she was in the wing of the new products division, sitting in the office of her friend Cindy Cooper. They had chatted for a few minutes about Cindy's upcoming marriage to her boss, Kyle Prentice, and Sophia's role as one of the bridesmaids in the wedding. Then, without preamble, Sophia had uncharacteristically blurted out the concerns weighing on her mind.

"Oh?" Cindy's green eyes sparkled. She leaned forward in her chair. "How can I help?"

Since turning thirty and transforming herself from a hard-driven career-oriented professional into a calm, confident woman who'd risked everything to find personal happiness, and had won, Cindy had become a true beauty. She wore her shoulder-length hair in a flattering blunt cut with soft wispy bangs fanning her forehead. She'd surrendered her austere business attire and sensible flat shoes for bold-colored, short-skirted suits and high heels. Sophia admired the changes in her friend, had in fact come to her office in order to quiz her about the role her metamorphosis had played in capturing the heart of Kyle Prentice.

"It's about Michael Barrington."

"Do tell." Cindy grinned. "I hear he's got a very sexy telephone voice."

"Yes, he does," Sophia admitted. "I just wish I knew what he looked like in person."

"You mean, does the face fit the voice?"

Sophia nodded. "You see, I've sort of got a crush on my boss."

"There's a lot of that going around." Cindy chuckled and waved her left hand, which sported an enormous engagement ring.

"That's what I need to ask your advice about," Sophia said, keeping her voice low.

"How to snare your boss?"

"Uh-huh."

"It's a touchy issue, mixing work and an office romance."

"But you and Kyle managed to pull it off."

Cindy chuckled. "It certainly wasn't easy. Kyle wasn't always so cooperative."

"What happened?"

"He didn't realize he was ready to fall in love."

"What changed his mind?" Sophia asked.

"Do you want to know what really worked for me?"

"Absolutely."

"I stopped caring."

Sophia frowned. "I don't understand."

"When I turned thirty, I realized that life was passing me by. I was sitting at my desk every day, waiting for Kyle to really notice me as a woman but he never did. Oh sure, he told me I was a great secretary. He complimented my organizational skills, but he never saw me as a desirable woman until I stopped caring what he thought and started living life for myself."

"What are you saying?"

"Stop holding your breath waiting for Michael Barrington to come home and sweep you off your feet."

"But Cindy, you don't understand. I've *got* to have Michael. I can't stop trying."

"Why?"

"Why what?"

"Why do you have to have him?"

"Cindy, Michael is kind and considerate, hardworking and dependable. He's everything I ever needed in a man, and I care for him deeply."

"But if he's not crazy about you, what's the point?" her friend asked. It was a good question.

"Michael *might* be crazy about me. It's hard to tell when he's so far away."

"Has he said or done anything that led you to believe your relationship was anything other than professional?"

"Well," Sophia considered the question. Michael was friendly and nice but she couldn't say that he was exactly flirtatious. "He sent me flowers for my birthday."

Cindy nodded her approval. "That's a start. Still, don't let this stop you from going out and having a good time with other men. After all, he's in Germany and you're here. You're young and beautiful. You should be having the time of your life."

Her friend didn't understand. She didn't know about Jannette and the fear of physical intimacy she had instilled in Sophia. Because of her mother's influence, Sophia had difficulty even dating, much less having the "time of her life."

"I don't want to go out with any other men," Sophia protested. Except Michael!

"There are billions of men in the world. If Michael isn't the one for you, another one will come along."

But no one else that was so perfect for her. Not a man who could make all her dreams come true. Dreams that roving Mike the mailman could never fulfill. Dreams that included safety and security as well as love and affection.

"Your attitude is holding you back," Cindy continued. "As long as I sat around mooning about Kyle, he never worried about me. He knew I would be there. But when I took charge of things and got on with my life, he realized there was a chance some other guy might snatch me up. Let me tell you, Sophia, the man did a complete one-eighty. Try not caring. You'll be amazed at what happens."

Easy for Cindy to say. She and her boss had been together in the same office day in and day out. Kyle had witnessed Cindy's transformation. But with Michael, Sophia faced a completely different problem. How could they bond without proximity? How could she make Michael jealous when he was thousands of miles away? How would he even know if she was living her own life or waiting pitifully by the phone?

"I better get back to work," Sophia said, rising to her feet. "Thanks for the advice."

"Anytime, but hey, I also wanted to give you a word of warning."

"Oh?"

"It's about Mike the mailman."

"Mike?"

"Yes. Nick Delaney saw the two of you riding on Mike's motorcycle last night."

"Don't jump to conclusions, Cindy. Mike was simply giving me a ride home."

"Just be careful. Okay? Even though I'm advising you to stop caring about Michael Barrington, I don't know if Mike is the right person to stop caring about him with, if you get my drift."

Sophia frowned. "Why not?"

"Mike has got a bit of a reputation."

"Reputation?"

"You know." Cindy lowered her voice. "Kyle says he's a real womanizer. I also hear he likes to party a little too hearty."

"I don't think Mike is like that."

"I'd hate to see you get hurt, Sophia. Don't fall for the bad boys. They can't be changed."

"I'm not falling for Mike." She spoke with more force than she intended, as if trying to convince herself as well as Cindy. "My cap is set for Michael Barrington."

"All right, then. Good luck."

"Thanks."

Great. Cindy hadn't been much help. On the one hand she advised Sophia not to put her life on hold for Michael Barrington, but on the other she specifically warned her away from Mike the mailman.

What was a girl to do?

Sighing, Sophia wandered back to her office thinking she might just give up on men entirely.

Chapter Five

"Ready to call it a day?"

The moment she'd been dreading for hours had arrived. Sophia grasped the edges of her desk so tightly that her knuckles whitened.

"Hello, Mike," she greeted him coolly.

Despite her best efforts to quell her libido, the minute she spotted Mike lounging casually with his shoulder against the wall, one corner of his mouth quirked up in a knowing grin, her heart leapfrogged painfully against her rib cage.

Don't look at me like that!

He appeared so deliciously handsome with a thick lock of hair laying across his forehead, Sophia imagined that Michael Barrington never looked so carefree. Of course not. He was a man with a lot of responsibility. He didn't have time to waste. He had a multimillion-dollar business to run. Mike the mailman could afford to be disarmingly boyish. He had nothing else going for him beyond his looks and his charm. Sophia would not fall for it. She had told Michael she was loyal to him and she meant it. No matter how tempting Mike the mailman might be, she had to clip this budding relationship before it had a chance to flourish and destroy them both. Especially since she'd finally managed to snare Michael Barrington's interest.

"Nice flowers," Mike commented, sauntering across the room with his easy swagger. Sophia decided that Michael never swaggered. She supposed he strode purposefully into a room, instantly commanding everyone's attention.

Mike bent over and smelled the flowers. "Very nice. Where'd they come from?"

"Mr. Barrington sent them to me for my birthday."

"That was very nice of Rex," Mike said.

"They're from Michael," she corrected him.

"Oh." Straightening, Mike pressed his lips together in a disapproving line. "Makes my glass kitten look sort of pathetic, doesn't it?"

"No, Mike." Sophia immediately felt contrite for having gloated over the flowers. She adored that little glass kitten and it had been sweet of Mike to give it to her. She just didn't want to lead him on and let him think they had a chance to be more than friends when they did not. "I love that kitten."

He made a face. "It's okay. You don't have to lie to spare my feelings."

"I'm not lying," she snapped. What was it about this man? He was either sweeping her off her feet or irritating the hell out of her.

"Never mind." He raised his palms. "Are you ready to head for home?"

"Er…" She'd spent the entire afternoon trying to think of an excuse to get out of giving him a ride home. "I have so much work to catch up on. How about I spring for a taxi?"

"Don't worry about it. I can wait. I've got nowhere else to be."

That, Sophia thought, was the crux of Mike's problem. He had no plans, no structure, no ambition. But she kept her opinion to herself. Instead she said, "I could be hours." She didn't like lying to him, but her survival was at stake.

"I'll wait."

Great! What now? She had to get rid of him. The last thing she wanted or needed was to be left in the building alone with this man whom she found so devilishly attractive. A man who could ruin her chances with the guy she really wanted.

"Mike, I'm sure you'd rather go home and have your supper. Really, I don't mind paying for your taxi. I owe you after you fixed my car."

He pushed the flowers aside and nonchalantly hopped up to sit on her desk. "You need to eat, too." He reached for the phone. "I'll call for pizza. What kind do you like?"

Sophia stared. He winked at her.

"Pepperoni," she said helplessly.

"How do you feel about mushrooms?"

She nodded.

"Green peppers? Black olives?"

"Get the works." She laughed. "But no anchovies."

"Gotcha." He pointed his finger like a gun and pulled an imaginary trigger.

Yes, you do.

He dialed the number to a pizza delivery service. She sighed and sank down into her chair. The guy did not take no for an answer. Fine. He could sit there and be bored to death while she worked.

Except Sophia was all caught up and had absolutely nothing to work on.

What if one of their co-workers came by, she fretted,

and caught them having pizza together in her office? That would only add fuel to the already flaming office grapevine. And what if Michael got wind of this innocent tryst? Would he think she had lied to him about having someone special in her life?

Sophia winced.

"Something wrong?" Mike cocked his head inquisitively, giving him an endearing quality.

You.

His gaze snared hers. He leaned closer across her desk. His tangy scent caught her nose, tantalized her. His warm breath lightly tickled her skin.

Sophia realized with a jolt that he'd splashed on fresh cologne before coming into her office. Was he trying to seduce her with his intoxicating aroma?

He narrowed his gaze. Sophia noticed his eyes had turned a darker shade of green, murkier, colored by desire. Her glance traveled down his face, caught and paused at his mouth.

The mouth that had caused her so much trouble.

Would Michael Barrington kiss like Mike the mailman? Would his lips send red-hot rockets shooting to her toes? Or would they be soft and gentle? Would his mouth be hot and hard like Mike's or kind and understanding?

Which did she prefer? Fireworks or comfort?

"See something you like?" Mike asked, his sexy voice rasping against her eardrums, driving her crazy.

Sophia yanked her eyes from his face and stared down at her desk. She felt her pulse quicken at her neck. Was the man a magician or a mind reader or both?

"You're in my way." She pointed at a sky-blue chair located halfway across the room. "Go sit over there."

He smirked but did not move.

"Shoo." She motioned him away with both hands.

Still he didn't go.

"I can't work with you staring at me like that. If you don't want to spend the night here with me, I suggest you get off my desk and let me get this stuff taken care of."

"I'd spend the night with you anywhere, Sophia."

She did not want to blush! Oh, no! But her cheeks heated anyway.

"Why are you so shy? You're a beautiful woman." Mike reached over and took her hand.

"Please don't," she whispered. "What if someone passes by in the corridor and sees us?"

"What if they do?"

"We'll be the talk of the office."

"So? Let them talk. I don't care. Do you?"

Sophia wrenched her hand from his. "Yes. I do care. Very much. And that is exactly the reason I can't become involved with you, Mike. You don't care. About your job, the impression you make on people, anything."

That seemed to sober him for a moment. He drew back and slanted her a sultry look. Her heart leapt into her throat.

"Is that the real reason, Sophia, or is it because you're determined to marry Michael Barrington and don't want to blow your chances by dating me?"

She sat up straight, and even though it took every ounce of courage she possessed, Sophia stared him in the eye. "I care for Michael a great deal, yes."

"Tell me something." He reached out to caress her cheek with one finger. "If I were the rich one, the one with all the money and cars and homes, would you forget all about Michael Barrington?"

"No," Sophia said sharply, but she feared it was true.

No man had ever set her body ablaze the way Mike did. She wanted him desperately. Her body ached for him twice as much as her heart longed to be Mrs. Rex Michael Barrington III. But Mike wasn't rich, he wasn't ambitious. He could not provide for a family. He had no desire to settle down. He liked to play and party just as her father had. How could she choose a man like that? She could not, would not follow in her mother's footsteps and fall into bed with a man simply because her hormones were raging.

And yet she wanted him! Blindly, stupidly, with every fiber of her being.

"Are you telling me the truth, Sophia?" He lowered his head and his voice. "You seriously find that uptight Harvard graduate more attractive than me?"

"Attraction has nothing to do with it."

"Sweetheart," Mike said, and that single word sent a shaft of delight arrowing through her. "Attraction has everything to do with it. Deny that what happened in your car this morning was anything less than earth-shattering."

"I don't base important decisions on the surge of passion," Sophia replied primly. "I prefer to rationalize my choices with a well-thought-out plan of action."

"You think too much," he said, moving closer until mere inches separated them. Just when Sophia feared Mike was going to kiss her, the pizza delivery boy showed up, bringing with him the smell of yeast and tomato sauce.

Grateful for the interruption, Sophia hopped up from her chair and smiled at her teenage savior. She rummaged in her purse then extended the delivery boy a twenty-dollar bill. He swapped her the pizza and some change.

She watched the delivery boy go with lingering anxiety. Two seconds later she was left alone again with Mike.

"I'll go for sodas," Mike said. "Diet cola, right?"

She nodded.

Mike left Sophia's office and went to catch the elevator to the break room. What did he want from Sophia? he asked himself as he strolled the hallway, his hands in his front pockets.

He wanted her to want him for himself. Not his money.

Not his name. Not for the stability he could provide. He wanted to know that *he,* ordinary Mike, could please her without having to be Rex Michael Barrington III, successful corporate executive. He wanted to be responsible for putting a smile on her face and a song in her heart. He wanted to make her moan with delight. He wanted for her to call his name in ecstasy.

But Sophia resisted his every effort, so hung up was she with the thought of marrying her boss.

Mike wandered into the break room, fed quarters into the soft drink machine.

She was such a sexy woman. She carried herself with a calm confidence. Like Cleopatra or a much-sought-after movie star. He knew her potent sexuality was natural, not some put-on. He also knew she did not know how to deal with the desires she unintentionally raised in men.

What should he do? Give up pursuing her? And turn his back on what could possibly be the love of his life? Mike wasn't getting any younger, and lately, whenever he gazed at Sophia, he experienced the most overwhelming longings that included weddings and honeymoons, babies and happily-ever-after.

Yes. He was falling for her. But was she falling for him?

He could, of course, reveal his true identity. She'd sure as heck want him and then he'd never know for sure if she loved him for himself, or if, like his ex-fiancée, Erica, she was simply seeking a trophy husband.

Mike winced.

There was really only one alternative. And it was a dangerous one. He must seduce her as Mike the mailman and yet he had to keep a firm grip on his own emotions in case she did turn out to be like Erica. Mike never wanted to go through pain like that again. But Sophia was worth the risk. If she could surrender herself to a man she believed too irresponsible and unambitious, if she could give up her desperate need for security in order to obtain real love, then and only then would he know the truth.

Sophia heard him coming down the corridor. The building was silent except for his footsteps.

Her heart thumped in response—wham, wham, wham.

Dammit, but she wanted him. Wanted his kisses, his hands on her skin, his body pressed against hers.

When he was near, Mike dominated her senses, wove his spell, made her forget all about Michael Barrington and her vow to woo and win her boss.

No matter how illogical it was, her body longed to be joined with Mike. The man from the mail room. The here-today, gone-tomorrow rolling stone who could promise her nothing.

Despite all that, she still wanted him.

Remember what happened to your mother!

The sad tale Jannette had narrated a thousand times throughout Sophia's childhood rang with brilliant clarity. She could not depend upon her heart to lead her in the right direction. If she followed her body's basic urgings, and allowed herself to make love with Mike, what then? Did they have a future together? What if she got pregnant? Would he run out on her the way her father had abandoned her mother? Or worse, would he feel obligated to marry her, but be unwilling to make a real career for himself. Would she and the baby be forced to live in the sort of poverty she'd grown up in and had vowed never to bring a child into?

Use your head, Sophia. Forget you have a heart. One of Jannette's frequent phrases spun through her mind. *Hearts are made for breaking, heads for thinking.*

Mike's footsteps quieted on the carpet. He carried two soda cans and paper plates.

Sophia looked up. Her breath left her body. He was so incredibly handsome!

She had to get out of here, run away from him before she did something too stupid to consider.

His body filled the doorway, blocking her escape. Sophia gulped, startled at her physical reaction to him. Desire stole over her like an illness. Her palms were slick with perspiration, her brow feverish. She felt dizzy and her stomach fluttered.

Who was this man who affected her like no other? Even when she tried to focus on Michael Barrington, to mentally list his good qualities, she could not concentrate while looking at Mike.

She knew almost nothing about him save he had a reputation for partying and he rode a motorcycle. He had a killer grin and a nonchalant way of walking that made her want to jump his bones. Beyond that, she had no knowledge of the man. Not who his folks were, nor where he came from. She had no idea what his dreams were, his hopes, his plans for the future, if indeed he even possessed any. She didn't know his favorite color or his favorite food.

Strangely enough, she knew all these things about Michael Barrington even though she didn't know what *he* looked like. Over the past four months these little details had come up in conversation, or in e-mail posts.

Michael was the only child of Rex Michael Barrington II who had built the Barrington Corporation from the ground up back in the sixties. His mother had been Freda Heidler Barrington, originally from West Germany. That was the reason Michael spoke fluent German. His mother had died fifteen years ago of breast cancer and her death had struck Michael a hard blow. In reaction, Michael had poured himself into the company, opening and overseeing the European division. His dream was to take his father's corporation and turn it into the largest hotel chain in the world. He wanted a wife and children someday. His favorite color was cherry red and his favorite dish was lamb chops with mint jelly, glazed carrots, new potatoes and green beans. He liked jogging, in-line skating and baseball. He was steady, reliable and an excellent provider. What more could anyone ask for?

Chemistry.

Just like the power surging between her and Mike, right here, right now.

"Sophia," Mike said softly. She knew he felt it, too.

Too bad both men couldn't be one and the same, Sophia thought regretfully. Everything she'd ever wanted rolled into one package. Hot good looks and a steady personality. A rebel with a future.

But she could not have both. Life wasn't that kind. Mike was Mike and Michael was Michael. Even if they shared a common name, they were two very different men.

And Mike was the one gazing at her with a desire so strong, she felt as if her clothing was being torn from her body by his bold stare.

A long moment stretched into painful silence.

"Are you afraid of me?" Mike asked at last, still standing in the doorway clutching the cola and paper plates, the smell of onions and garlic wafting in the air around them.

"Don't be silly," Sophia said, but she refused to look at him. "Why would I be afraid of you?"

"Because you're so darn attracted to me you don't know what to do about it."

Was she afraid of him? Or was she afraid of herself and the feelings that threatened to riot and overthrow her good sense?

He stalked across the room, set his burden on her desk, then shut the office door tightly closed. He turned around to challenge her.

"Are you afraid you like me more than you like Barrington?" he asked. "Are you worried that what you feel for me disturbs the neat little scenario you've got planned for your life?"

Afraid, no, terrified, yes.

"Let's eat," Sophia chirped, anxious to derail this particular topic of conversation. She reached for the pizza box but he stopped her by placing a hand on her arm.

"You didn't answer my question." His fingers splayed across her skin, branding her with the intensity of his touch.

"No," she denied. How could she admit her weakness to him, when she scarcely dared admit it to herself?

"Then kiss me, Sophia. Prove to me that I don't drive you crazy with desire."

"Mike..." she began but got no further.

"Deny this, Sophia Shepherd."

He grabbed both her wrists and pulled her flush against his chest. He stared into her face, gobbling her up with his moss-green eyes.

Sophia gasped. Shocked but excited.

His mouth swooped down on hers like a nighthawk claiming its helpless prey—powerful, strong, demanding.

It made the kiss in the car seem like a grandparent's affectionate peck on the cheek.

Push him away! her mind urged. *Now. Before it's too late.*

But her rebellious body disobeyed her warnings. She did not care about chastity or restraint. She craved satisfaction like a dieter craved chocolate-chip cookies. Tossing all caution into the face of that raging tornado that was her accelerating passion, Sophia melted into Mike, molding herself around his hard form, pressing as close to him as she could get.

He groaned and clutched her tighter.

Sophia arched her neck upward, exposing her throat to his hungry mouth.

His firm, masculine hands pulled her blouse from the waistband of her pants. He slowly, seductively unbuttoned the garment, his nimble fingers grazing her bare skin.

A trail of fire.

He kept exploring, gently pushing aside her bra until he discovered the prize he had been searching for.

Her nipples beaded instantly against his touch. He strummed them softly with his thumbs. The sensation was exquisite.

Sophia hissed in her breath. Her groin ached with a heaviness that begged release.

Mike buried his face in her hair. "Sophia," he whispered. "Sophia, Sophia, Sophia."

Her name sounded so beautiful tripping from his tongue. She savored his sweet utterance, committing it to memory.

Like mountaineers scaling Mount Everest, they climbed the peak of passion together. Higher, harder, faster their need escalated as they drank thirstily from each other's parched lips.

Mike eased her backward as if they were dancing until he pressed her securely against the wall. His tongue plunged deep, exploring the cave of her mouth, while his hand still tenderly massaged her breasts.

Sophia never fought, never argued with his trespass. She allowed him full entry, courted his deep-throated kiss.

Day was night. Night was day. She lost all sense of time, all reason or rhyme. Nothing mattered but him. His touch. His smell. His taste.

His head descended, low, then lower still. A hundred kisses fell from his lips to her chin, her neck, the hollow of her throat and beyond.

The next thing she knew he had dropped to his knees and was eye level with her chest.

Sophia gasped when she realized his intention. Groaning, she arched her back and splayed her palms against the cool tile walls.

His tongue, hot and wet, flicked tantalizingly over her straining pink buds.

His actions sent daggers stabbing into her groin, increasing her delicious agony. Inside, she grew damp.

Sophia caught a glimpse of their reflection in the window. She was writhing against the wall, her blouse hanging open, Mike on his knees suckling at her breast.

What would Jannette say if she could see her daughter now? The thought grabbed Sophia and shook her. How many years had Jannette preached against such behavior? How often had she been warned that the price of runaway lust was simply too high to pay.

Oh, dear, what was she doing? She had to stop this now, before there was no turning back.

But the impulse to cease her activities came and went unheeded. The pleasure was simply too great to be denied. It was as if Sophia were glued to that wall, helpless to move or change the course of her destiny.

Instead, she peered down at the top of Mike's head. His hair was so thick and brown, like a field of chocolate. Reaching out, she threaded her fingers in it.

She laughed with the joy.

All these years this is what she had been missing by holding herself back, remaining wary, honoring Jannette's experiences and making them her own. She had been wrong and foolish.

Sophia closed her eyes and breathed deeply.

"Oh, Michael." She sighed. "That feels so good."

As if he'd been doused with ice water, Mike instantly ceased what he was doing.

"I'm Mike," he said coldly, pulling back from her and staggering to his feet.

Sophia's eyes flew open. "Oh, Mike, I'm sorry. I..." She reached out to him, but he shunned her.

"No need to explain. I know Barrington is the one you were fantasizing about." Mike looked hurt. Wounded. "The one you really want."

"That's not true!" she denied.

"Oh, spare me." Mike's chest rose and fell angrily. "No matter how much you might want to make love to me, you can't get over Michael Barrington's checkbook, can you?"

Tears stung her eyes. Blindly Sophia fumbled with the buttons on her blouse.

The only person she'd been thinking of was Mike. If she'd said Michael, it had been purely by accident. Their names were so similar, it was a natural mistake.

He spun on his heels and stalked away from her.

"Wait," she cried. "How are you going to get home?"

"Don't worry about me, Sophia. I can take care of myself."

"Please, don't go. I didn't mean to hurt you."

Mike threw a cold glare at her over his shoulder then flung open the door.

What they saw startled them both.

Rex Michael Barrington II stood in the hallway, an expression of surprise etched across his kindly features.

Chapter Six

"Mike." Rex Barrington nodded at them. "Sophia."

"Mr.—Mr.—Barrington," she stammered.

Mike looked pale.

"I heard noises," Mr. Barrington said. "I didn't realize you were here late, Sophia."

"Yes, sir."

Rex Barrington glanced at his watch and frowned. "That son of mine isn't working you too hard, is he?"

"No, sir." She blushed, ashamed at having been caught. Alone with Mike. After hours. With her office door closed.

Mike squirmed self-consciously and studied the floor. Sophia couldn't blame him. As disheveled as they both appeared, it left little doubt what they had been up to.

"You working late too, Mike?"

Was it her imagination or was Mr. Barrington struggling hard not to grin? Did he find their situation amusing? That surprised her.

"No, sir, I'm off the clock. Sophia was going to give me a lift home," Mike explained.

"Why don't you go ahead and call it a day," Rex suggested. "The work will still be here tomorrow."

"Yes, sir."

"Have a good night." He smiled.

"Good night," she and Mike mumbled in unison.

"That," Mike said, once Rex was out of hearing distance, "was a very close call."

"Too close for comfort." Sophia exhaled loudly. Her hands trembled as she ran them through her hair, fighting desperately to smooth her errant curls. "Listen, Mike, about what happened earlier, I'm sorry I called you Michael."

He shrugged. "Don't worry about it."

"No, seriously, I apologize."

"You really want to make it up to me?" he asked, casting her a sideways glance.

Sophia cleared her throat. "Er...what do you have in mind?"

"Go with me to the company picnic next month."

"I can't."

"Why not? Because Michael Barrington is going to be there?" His tone was sarcastic.

"Where did you hear that Michael was going to be there?"

"Office rumors."

Sophia stared at him, unconvinced. Could Mike have possibly eavesdropped on her conversation with Michael? The thought infuriated her. There was no doubt in her mind that he was jealous of Michael. She wouldn't put it past him.

"I'm going home," she said, getting her purse from the bottom of her desk. "Good luck getting a ride."

With that, she turned and stalked out the door.

* * *

Mike couldn't sleep. His condo seemed claustrophobic, the walls closing in on him.

His body was hot, fevered with the memory of Sophia's kisses. He recalled the taste of her delicious breasts and moaned low in his throat. She'd felt so good in his arms. So right.

Then why was he lying here empty-handed?

She'd been angry at him, but Mike found her anger exciting. Anger meant she cared.

He flopped over on his side and stared at the digital radio clock on the dresser. Ten-thirty. Had only four hours passed since he'd last seen Sophia? It felt like forty.

Why did he care so much? After all, she had called him Michael. The name of his wealthy alter ego.

No matter how much he turned her on. No matter how high their combined temperatures had climbed. No matter how much she had wanted him—simple Mike the mailman—Sophia had been unable to erase Michael Barrington from her mind.

Why?

She'd never met the man. She didn't know how she would react to him in person. She had only interacted with her boss over the computer, over the phone, through the mail. How could she be in love with him?

Fool. She's in love with his money. His status. His power. That's what Sophia wants. Not the love of a poor man.

Love.

The word echoed in his head creating a strange, aching sensation inside Mike's chest.

Was he in love with Sophia Shepherd?

No. He shook his head, denying his feelings. How could he be in love with a woman who could not love him back? A woman who wanted only what he could provide. A woman who would ignore her instincts in favor of her cool calculating mind.

It's happened before.

The memory floated to him out of the darkness and wrapped painfully around his heart.

Erica.

Blonde like Sophia and beautiful, too. But with a conniving heart of solid granite.

He'd met her in his wild-boy phase, when he'd temporarily dropped out of college to spite Rex. He'd been traveling the country on his motorcycle, exploring his "bad" side. It had been an unforgettable adventure, one of the few times he hadn't been judged for his money because he'd pretended to be poor. People accepted him for himself and for a little while he'd let his guard slip. Then he'd met Erica, accidentally running into her on the ski slopes in Park City, Utah. At least he'd thought their meeting had been accidental. He'd even joked about how fate had smiled on him that day, delivering such an angel into his arms. It was only later, after he had invested his emotions into Erica, that Mike had discovered that the fall she'd taken had been carefully orchestrated and timed to happen just as he skied by. Lady Luck had not brought them together. Erica had. His ruse had not fooled her. Somehow she had discovered he wasn't really a wild-boy biker but was instead the son of a rich hotel magnate. And Erica wasn't an angel, either, rather the opposite.

He'd been young and dumb. He'd thought himself head over heels for Erica. They'd even planned their wedding. He'd told her who he was by then and she'd acted surprised but pleased. And then one day he'd overheard her on the phone talking to her mother. She'd been laughing and gloating over her good fortune to be marrying a millionaire. She'd belittled him. Calling him stupid and gullible.

Even though it had happened sixteen years earlier, the betrayal still hurt. He rejected Erica and broke off their engagement. When his mother died, Erica came to the funeral on the arm of a famous billionaire twice her age. She'd shown up not to comfort Mike in his time of need, but to flaunt her new husband in his face. Mike hadn't cared. He'd been so grief stricken over the loss of his mother. He'd simply felt sorry for the billionaire, who despite his money, obviously led a shallow life. Following his mother's death, he had put the Harley in storage, mended fences with his father, went back to school and pitched himself into the business with a fevered vengeance. If money was what everyone valued, by God, he'd show them money.

Mike gritted his teeth and shoved the memory to the back of his mind. Erica had taught him an important lesson about letting his heart lead his head. And for the most part, he'd learned his lesson well, always keeping himself above the messy fray of emotions.

Until now.

Until Sophia.

She isn't like Erica, his conscience prodded. She's different. Sophia is warm and friendly. Kind and understanding. She's honest and open with no hidden agenda.

But she, like Erica, wanted to marry a rich man. Except Sophia hadn't kept her motives a secret. She'd made it clear from the start that security was the most important thing in life. After seeing how she lived, Mike could understand her position.

Give her a chance.

But hadn't he already? More than once. Sophia had turned down his invitation to the picnic because she knew Michael Barrington was going to be there and she didn't dare risk having her boss believe that she had a boyfriend.

Wasn't that proof enough?

No. Because for a few minutes tonight, when they were alone in her office, Sophia had completely forgotten about Michael Barrington. For a few minutes of pure bliss, she had belonged to Mike the mailman, mind, body and soul.

She could not have faked her response to him. Her gorgeous body had come alive at his touch, opening like a flower bud to a gentle spring shower. She wanted him. Needed him. Lusted after him with a frightening intensity that had swept away caution. He'd tasted passion on her tongue, smelled heated desire on her skin.

Mike groaned. He grew hard just thinking about her.

So was he going to lay here all night, fighting sleep, or was he going to get up and do something about it?

Frustration had him flinging back the covers and sinking his feet into the carpet. He had to shake Sophia from his head. Had to regain his perspective on this relationship and where it might be leading. He knew only one cure for emotional craziness.

The Harley beckoned.

He had to ride.

"Rachel," Sophia said into the phone. She lay on her stomach in the middle of her bed, clothed in pajamas. She rotated her legs in the air. It was after ten o'clock and Jannette had already gone to bed. "I desperately need another opinion on this situation. Olivia thinks I should give Mike a chance. My mother, of course, believes I should keep my sights fixed firmly on Michael Barrington. Cindy told me to forget them both and start living it up. I'm so confused!"

"What does your heart tell you?" Rachel said simply.

"I don't know," Sophia whispered. Rachel was such a centered person, with a calm inner strength Sophia admired. If Rachel couldn't help her get a handle on this situation, no one could.

"Then get quiet and listen."

"It's not that simple," Sophia protested.

"Yes it is."

"How do I do that?"

"Take a few deep breaths, relax, lay still."

"Yes?"

"Think about what it is you really want," Rachel coached.

"Okay."

"Do it right now."

"All right."

"I'll see you at work tomorrow," her friend said. "You tell me how it worked out."

"Good night, Rachel. Thanks for listening."

"Anytime."

Sophia hung up the phone, then turned off the lamp. She lay spread eagle across the bedspread and took several long, slow deep breaths. Instantly Sophia felt herself relaxing as the concerns of the day began to dissipate and fall away.

"Relax," she chanted with each breath.

Before she knew it, she was floating on an invisible cloud. She closed her eyes and in her mind she saw Mike. Her heart beat faster.

He smiled at her.

Who did she want? Mike with his ready grin, sexy body and fun personality or Michael with his good business sense, sensuous phone voice and practical nature?

Listen to your heart.

What did she want?

It wasn't money she craved, Sophia realized. Not really. Rather it was the fairy-tale ending of happily-ever-after that having money seemed to imply. She didn't care if Mike was rich or not. That was not the point. What she wanted was a man she could count on. One that would not abandon her in her time of need the way her father had abandoned her mother. One who would not lie to her. As long as Mike could take responsibility and become a man, if he could stop running, stop playing at being Peter Pan and settle down, then he was the one she truly wanted.

There was no denying her response to him.

He stirred something deep and primordial within her. He was man. She was woman. She ached for the two of them to be joined.

It felt right, but could she truly trust her feelings?

"Sophia?"

She heard her mother call out in the darkness. Sighing, Sophia opened her eyes and got off the bed without having found the answers she so desperately sought.

"Yes, Mother?" Sophia padded into her mother's bedroom, guided by the night-light. She found Jannette sitting up in bed, her hair in disarray. "Are you all right?"

"I had a bad dream."

Sophia slipped between the covers, got in bed beside her mother and curled up next to her. "What about?"

"I dreamed you left me."

"Mother, I'll never leave you."

"You're going to get married soon. I can feel it," Jannette said, holding Sophia close. "I'm scared."

"Shhh. Even if I get married I'll still be around."

"Will you?" Jannette sounded childlike.

"Of course."

"What if you decided to run off with that mailman?"

"Oh, Mother."

"You like him. I can tell."

"Yes," Sophia admitted.

"He's no good for you," Jannette whispered. "He'll only get you into trouble. I know about lust. I know what can happen."

"Mom, we've had this discussion a million times."

"You were with him tonight, weren't you?"

Sophia was tempted to deny it, but she never lied to her mother. Jannette had always taught her that honesty was the best policy and that advice had never steered her wrong.

"Yes."

"Oh, no," she gasped.

"Relax, Mother. I can handle Mike."

Jannette clutched the tail of Sophia's pajama top in her hand. "How can I relax? I want you to understand how important it is that you don't let some bad boy ruin your life. I thought I loved your father. I thought he loved me. But it was just sex! For him at least. I rebelled against my parents because they told me I couldn't date him. I thought I knew best. I was wrong."

"That was so long ago."

"Almost thirty years. But your father left me. And then I found out he was already married! He lied to me. Then he told me to have an abortion! Can you believe that? Later, when I heard he was killed in Vietnam, I didn't even cry. My parents were so ashamed, they sent me away. How could I blame them? I had been such a silly little fool, following my heart, believing a man who lied to me."

"But things were different for you, Mother. You were only seventeen. You didn't know any better."

"Maybe not. But I kept you and I raised you on my own. I worked two jobs to survive. I cut coupons, I traded baby-sitting services with my friends. I made do with little to nothing."

"And you did a wonderful job." Sophia gently kissed her mother's cheek. And she had. Despite her flaws, Jannette was a loving parent.

The tragedy of her mother's tale never failed to move Sophia. It was too sad. She'd been a young girl so blinded by love, she'd been unable to see Sophia's father for what he really was. She'd followed her heart and had been terribly disappointed. But the truly sad part was that she'd never forgiven the man. She'd never gotten past the old hurt and anger. She refused to let herself care about any man, ever again. She'd allowed resentment to build inside her to the point where she developed high blood pressure. Jannette had never spent money on herself, had always put Sophia's needs first. She did not go to the doctor even when the headaches had gotten progressively worse.

And then, at age thirty-seven Jannette had suffered a stroke so severe, it had rendered her left arm and leg permanently affected.

"Please, baby," Jannette sobbed softly. "Please don't let Mike fool you. You like him too much. I can see it in your face. It's just the way I felt over your father."

Was it true? Was she that easy to read?

"Shhh." Sophia gathered her mother in her arms and gently rocked her back and forth like a child. "It's all right. I'm always here for you, just like you were always there for me. Now go to sleep."

Several minutes passed. Jannette's breathing deepened. Sophia slipped out from under the covers.

She thought she heard a noise outside the house. Like the idling of a motorcycle engine.

Curious, Sophia returned to her room, plucked her bathrobe from a corner post on the bed and went to the living room window. She raised the curtain and peered out.

Moonlight bathed the street in a soft glow but it lay empty. No cars. No motorcycles.

Sophia dropped the curtain and moved to unlatch the front door. She stepped out onto the front porch. A slight breeze blew. She cinched the belt of her robe tighter, inhaled the scent of lemons in the air.

Crickets chirped from the cholla garden. Moths circled the street lamp, hungry for the flame. In the distance, a dog barked. Shu-Shu rubbed against her leg. Sophia picked up the cat, held her to her chest.

An ugly reminder from her childhood flashed through Sophia's mind, resurrecting an old hurt.

She had been nine years old and in the fourth grade when the most popular girl in school, Alice Anne Aubrey, invited the whole class to her house for a birthday party. Sophia had been so happy and excited. Jannette had taken her to the dime store to buy a gift for Alice Anne. Sophia had insisted on a Barbie doll even though it was out of their budget. But she had wanted so badly to be Alice Anne's friend that Jannette had conceded. They'd wrapped the doll in brightly colored paper and Jannette had dyed one of Sophia's old dresses so it would look new for the party.

For the first time in her life, Sophia had been invited by a popular kid to participate in something. She'd been so nervous, so anxious to do everything right.

The appointed day arrived and Jannette drove her to the Aubreys' house in Windover Heights, in the most exclusive area of Phoenix. To Sophia, the house was a virtual mansion with a swimming pool and a tennis court. There were brightly colored balloons and streamers decorating the driveway. Sophia had walked up the stone pathway, her heart thudding with anticipation. Perhaps now Alice Anne would be nice to her and stop pulling her hair on the playground.

Sophia rang the bell. Alice Anne answered the door wearing a beautiful white lace and pink satin party dress, her usual entourage assembled around her.

"What are you doing here?" Alice Anne sniffed, curling up her nose with disdain.

Sophia extended the gift. "I'm coming to your party."

"Who invited *you?*" Alice Anne sneered.

"You did." Sophia gulped back tears. Her knees felt

watery. "You got up in front of the whole class and said everyone was invited."

"Everyone except *bastards*."

"But I brought you a present," Sophia whispered, the awful word Alice Anne had uttered cutting her like a knife.

"You don't belong here," Alice Anne said, roughly snatching the present away.

"Why?" Sophia had cried. "Why don't I belong?"

"Look at you." Alice Anne swept a disdainful hand at Sophia's handmade dress. "You look like a rag picker."

"Rag picker, rag picker," the other children chorused.

"And you don't even have a daddy," the cruel girl had continued. "Bet you were so ugly when you were born, he ran off and left you for the crows to pick your eyes out."

"No!" Sophia had denied.

"But even the crows wouldn't peck you," the girl gloated.

"Yeah," the other children jeered.

Tears streaming down her face, Sophia had turned down the steps and ran, the children's derisive laughter ringing in her ears. She'd gone back to the road and sat there for two hours waiting for Jannette to return. It had been the most humiliating event in Sophia's young life. She was a bastard. That meant she didn't have a daddy.

She stuck her thumb in her mouth and sucked, vowing when she had kids, she would make sure they had a daddy so no one could ever ridicule them.

"This," Jannette had said, afterward, trying hard to console Sophia, "is why you must never ever let a boy talk you into his bed until you are married. Do you understand?"

Sophia had nodded.

"Your father lied to me. He made promises he couldn't keep and then he left us."

"Why?"

"I don't know," Jannette had said bitterly.

"Did he think I was ugly?"

"Oh, sweetie, he never even saw you. You're not to blame. Not at all. But you must promise me one thing, Sophia."

"What thing, Mama?"

"When you grow up, you must marry a rich man who can take care of you. If you marry a man with lots of money, people like Alice Anne Aubrey won't make fun of you anymore. You will have a big house of your own and you can throw all the lavish birthday parties you want. Promise me that, Sophia."

"I promise, Mommy."

Shu-Shu meowed to be let down, jerking Sophia back to the present. Tears dampened the corner of her eyes and she brushed them away. The sound of a motorcycle engine rumbled close by.

She glanced across the road.

The Harley-Davidson pulled to a stop outside her front gate.

Sophia held her breath.

It was Mike.

Their gazes met. Held.

Her heart slowed curiously.

He looked like a black knight on a black charger sitting there in the moonlight, enticing her to come play, to be a bad girl.

No.

Sophia.

He never opened his mouth and yet he called to her, his eyes beseeching her to cross the yard and join him. She could hear his mental beckoning in her head.

She could not. She would not go to him. She owed it to herself, to her mother and to the child she once had

been to never lose sight of her goals. She would not be
destroyed by lust as Jannette had been. She would marry
a man who could provide her with all the things she never
had and so desperately wanted. One way or the other, she
was determined to win Michael Barrington's heart, and she
would not allow Mike, with his sexy smile and irresponsible ways to sway her from her goal. Swallowing hard
against the pain, Sophia turned her back on him and disappeared inside the house.

Chapter Seven

Why had he gone to Sophia's house? Mike asked himself. What had he hoped to gain from appearing outside her gate at midnight? Had he secretly been fantasizing that, overjoyed to see him, Sophia would fling her body on the back of his motorcycle and tell him to ride like the wind? Had he imagined a repeat performance of what had happened between them in her office? Had he been hoping, at least in some small corner of his heart, that she would declare her undying devotion to him and renounce her ridiculous infatuation with Michael Barrington?

No. Truthfully, his motivation had been much simpler than that.

He'd been unable to stop himself from going to her. She'd dominated his mind, eclipsed his good sense, shattered his self-control.

Helplessly Mike had been drawn to Sophia's house. It was as if Cupid himself had spirited the Harley to Sand Mesa Heights.

But obviously Cupid had been on a futile mission. Sophia was not interested in pursuing a relationship with him.

He knew she'd seen him. There was no mistaking it. When he'd driven up to find her standing on the porch staring at him, his pulse had thudded in his throat, excited by the sight of her in those thin, white cotton pajamas and robe.

For one magical instant, Mike had believed that she was going to walk up the stone path, push open the gate and step out into the street.

He'd held his breath.

Their eyes had met.

Then Sophia had made a conscious decision. He'd seen it in her eyes.

She'd purposefully turned her back on him and walked away.

Not one word of greeting, not a wave, not a smile.

Instead she'd offered a cold shoulder.

He hadn't mistaken the message. His stomach had snarled into a knot more tangled than the deception he'd been weaving since pretending to be Mike the mailman.

How could he hold Sophia accountable? He'd gotten himself into the fix. From the very first his father had been opposed to the idea of him cloaking his identity. Rex had said it would lead to misunderstandings and that the employees would resent not being trusted. But Michael, sure he was right, had insisted. Now he wondered about how prudent that choice had been. If he had listened to his father, this situation between him and Sophia would not be an issue.

Yes, but you wouldn't have the chance to find out conclusively if Sophia can love you for yourself, he reminded himself.

Sighing, Mike drove into the driveway of his condo. He depressed the button on his garage door opener and rolled the motorcycle inside.

He had no other alternative. If he wanted to find out

what was truly in Sophia's heart, he had to step back and give her breathing room. To withdraw and give her the opportunity to think things through. Mike could be patient. After all, he had all the time in the world.

Mike never mentioned his midnight motorcycle ride to her house. Nor did he speak of the sizzling kisses they'd shared in her office on Friday evening. In fact, he barely spoke to her at all. When he came for the mail, he mumbled a brief hello and left as quickly as possible.

Good, Sophia thought to herself by Wednesday of the week following their tête-à-tête. *He's realized how futile a relationship between us would be, so he's letting things cool off. Very good.*

So why did she feel so crummy?

Mike had obviously gotten the hint that she wasn't interested.

But was that the truth?

Sophia stared out her window at the Phoenix skyline and drew in a sharp breath. Absentmindedly, she tapped a pencil against her desk. It was for the best. Jannette did not want her involved with Mike. And how could she blame her mother? Mike was irresponsible and undisciplined. Sophia could never count on a man who had no ambitions, no hopes or dreams. No matter how handsome Mike might be or how fast her pulse raced whenever he entered the room, she could not depend on him. Ultimately that was what marriage came down to—having someone you could depend on. Someone who would always be honest with you, no matter what. Mike simply did not fit the bill.

Concentrate on Michael Barrington. He'll be home in less than two weeks.

Except instead of comforting her, that thought carried its own trepidation. Strangely enough, her boss hadn't called in to the office since last Friday. It was as if both men in her life were ignoring her.

What if Michael Barrington wasn't attracted to her? Or what if it turned out that she wasn't physically attracted to him?

Before her close encounter of the erotic kind with Mike the mailman, Sophia would have dismissed sexual compatibility as unimportant. But since last Friday night, when Mike's gentle hands and roving mouth had taught her the true meaning of arousal, she could no longer deny that chemistry was an essential ingredient of a loving relationship.

Olivia had been correct.

Now that Sophia had gotten a taste of the pleasures a man's body could offer, there was no going back. Her list of necessary requirements for a husband was growing longer and more difficult to fulfill.

But she refused to give up hope. In every other way, Michael Barrington was the perfect man. She'd know soon enough if they could past the sexual compatibility hurdle.

Sophia flipped her desk calendar over and marked through today's date. Ten more days until the company picnic. Ten more days before Michael Barrington came home. Ten more days until she knew for sure. Could he make her feel as attractive as Mike made her feel? Could Michael make her feel *wanted?*

In the meantime, she was grateful that Mike seemed to be avoiding her. It made things so much easier.

The phone rang.

Sighing, Sophia reached for it. "Michael Barrington's office. Sophia Shepherd speaking. How may I help you?"

The deep chuckle on the other end of the line set her heart to thumping. "You sound awfully serious this morning. Is something amiss, Sophia?"

"Mr. Barrington," she exclaimed.

"Wait a minute. What did I tell you to call me?"

"Michael." She grinned, and felt her cheeks turn pink.

"I'm calling to bring you up to speed on the Helsberg account. Ready to take notes?"

"Ready," Sophia assured him, amazed at how quickly her gloomy mood had lifted.

Michael launched into the details of their latest hotel acquisition while she furiously took notes. They conducted business for several minutes then, when she sensed a lull in the conversation, she dared to broach the question that had been on her mind all weekend.

"Have you cemented your plans for the company picnic?" she asked timidly. "Are you still planning to be home by next Saturday?"

"Got the plane tickets."

"Do you?" she breathed. "Really?"

"Really." He chuckled again. The sound heated her bones, melted her heart.

"Are you coming to meet everyone at the office before you go to the picnic?" she asked.

"No time. My plane doesn't get in until late Friday night."

"But," Sophia protested, "I won't know what you look like."

"I'll still be a mystery then."

"How will I recognize you?"

"I'll be wearing blue shorts and a white T-shirt," he said.

"Okay. I'll be watching for you."

"You're not anxious to meet me in person, are you?"

"A little," she confessed. "And nervous, too."

"There's nothing to be nervous about," he replied. "Unless you're hiding something from me."

Sophia's laugh was shaky. "What could I be hiding from you?"

"Everyone has a few skeletons in their closet, Sophia."

"Not everyone," she denied vehemently. Mike was not a skeleton. They hadn't done anything more than serious necking. "Do you have skeletons, Michael?"

"You bet I do," he whispered huskily, then rang off without another word.

Michael hung up the phone. He rose to his feet, folded his arms across his chest and walked over to the floor-length windows of his father's executive office. He stared out at the parking lot beyond. Soon, this would be his office, his domain, but for now, it still belonged to Rex, who was, at this very moment, leaning back in his swivel leather chair, studying him with a hard eye.

"What do you think is the best way to go about revealing my identity to the employees?" Mike asked.

"Call a meeting and I'll introduce you. But I'll warn you now, Michael, this isn't going to be easy. The employees have come to know you as Mike the mailman. Don't be surprised if they resent you for spying on them."

"Dad, it had to be done. If I hadn't gone undercover to study how the company works I would never have discovered that my ex-assistant was selling secrets to the competition or that Pete Randall in the stockroom had been stealing us blind for years."

"Your charade served its purpose," Rex said, "but I can't help wondering if it's not going to cost you more in the long run."

"What do you mean?" Michael asked sharply.

"The price of goodwill. By hiding your identity and circulating among the employees without their knowledge, they're going to feel like they can't trust you."

"Ha! I'm the one who can't trust them."

"I realize that," Rex said simply. "And it's your short-coming, not theirs."

Michael frowned and stared at his father. "What are you talking about?"

"You've got a problem with trust, son."

"I wonder why that is," Mike replied, unable to keep the sarcasm from his voice.

A pained expression crossed Rex's face. "I know I wasn't always there for you and I'll sorely regret it. But you've got to let go of the past. I've tried to make amends to you. This one character flaw is keeping you from becoming a truly great executive. You need to learn to delegate more. You can't do everything yourself."

"You're right," Michael admitted.

"I know I'm partly to blame. We rose up the social scale so quickly. I know there were a lot of kids who pretended to be your friend because of who you were. You never knew who to trust. I know that bothered you. I also know that Erica made things worse. But you can't go around being suspicious of everyone all the time. Sometimes you've simply got to trust people."

"There is absolutely nothing wrong with questioning motives, Dad. Everyone, no matter how nice, has a hidden agenda. Some might say you go to the opposite extreme, that you want people to like you so much that you'll turn a deaf ear to a bad situation."

Anger flared in Rex's dark green eyes. "I've learned a few things over the years about human nature son, things they don't teach you in Harvard Business School. You have to trust people until they give you a reason not to."

Michael sighed. It wasn't the first time they'd had this conversation. But if he were honest with himself wouldn't he admit that over the course of the past few months spent as Mike the mailman, he'd had actually enjoyed being spontaneous and carefree?

It was similar to the experiences of his rebellious days when he'd left home after a major argument with Rex. It had been fun, assuming a new persona, claiming the identity of a man who accepted people at face value. In a way, it was like reclaiming his youth, going back in time when his life consisted of something more than working to amass more money. As Mike, he'd found a level of acceptance he'd been unable to believe in as the boss's son. When he was Mike, he knew that everyone liked him for himself. Michael Barrington never enjoyed that luxury.

"Dad, it's one thing to put your faith in your employees, but it's something else to be so trusting that you allow them to rip you off."

"Maybe so." Rex shrugged. "But in just a few weeks, the problem is all yours. I will be relaxing on the beach in Maui."

"You've earned it."

"What about Sophia?" Rex asked. "When are you going to tell her? You can't just come to work one day and let her find Mike the mailman sitting in her boss's office."

"I don't know."

"You've got to tell her privately."

Michael blew out his breath. It would not be easy. "All right."

"A boss and his secretary have a special relationship," Rex said. "One that's usually built on trust. Don't be surprised if Sophia feels even more betrayed than everyone else."

"Why should she feel betrayed? I'm the one she's been plotting to marry."

"Don't judge her too harshly, Michael. In case you haven't noticed, marrying the boss has reached epic proportions in this company. We're all one big happy family and I for one happen to like things that way. Sophia just got caught up in the emotional sweep. Even Mildred's been getting ideas."

Michael's mouth dropped open in surprise. "Dad? Really? You and Mildred, an item?"

"Are you honestly surprised?" Rex asked, amusement written on his face. "Mildred's been my anchor ever since your mother died. I don't know what I would have done without her."

"Still, I never thought…"

"What's the matter, son? You think you young folks have a patent on love?" Rex grinned naughtily.

"Well, no. I think it's great, Dad. Congratulations." Michael strode across the room to pump his father's hand. "You deserve all the happiness life has to offer."

"So do you, son." Rex's face sobered. "That's why I've been lecturing you about trust. Until you can learn to trust a woman, you're never going to get married."

He did want to get married, Michael realized with a start. But he was afraid. Afraid of loving and not being loved in return. Afraid of losing that love once he found it, like his father had lost his mother. Afraid to trust, to let down his guard. And the only woman he desired was the one female he simply could not trust.

"You look very nice, Sophia," Jannette complimented her.

They drove along the highway, headed west toward the lake. The smell of fried chicken escaped from the picnic basket in the back seat.

"Thanks."

Sophia was dressed in blue denim skorts and a white cotton blouse. She had orchestrated for her clothing to mimic the outfit Michael planned to wear. Sophia had heard some psychologist on a radio call-in talk show say that men liked for their women to dress as they did. It was considered a sign of synergy.

She wore blue denim sneakers and short white socks

with pompoms at the back. She'd caught her hair into a ponytail with a large white bow. A thin gold chain adorned her neck and two gold studs were nestled in her earlobes.

"I'm so pleased I'm finally going to get to meet your boss."

"Me, too."

Sophia had dreamed of this moment for months. Her anxiety had mounted with each day that passed until now, on this bright, warm Saturday morning, she felt ready to explode with nervous anticipation. What would Michael look like? she wondered. Would he be as handsome as his father? How would he react? Would he hug her? Shake her hand? Would he smile sexily and flirt a little or would Michael be more reserved?

The official invitation from the Barrington Corporation to the annual end-of-the-summer fling had encouraged employees to bring family members along. Sophia didn't know whether her mother's presence would make things better or worse for her but after seeing the excitement in her mother's eyes at the thought of an outing, she was glad Jannette had come.

"I'm also very proud of you that you had the courage to break things off with Mike," Jannette said.

Break things off with Mike? He'd broken things off with her. Or so Sophia supposed. A strange ache lodged in her belly. He'd stopped hanging around her office, had even discontinued his hearty greetings when he made the mail rounds. She felt as if she'd lost her best friend.

"Let's not talk about Mike, okay?"

Jannette nodded and reached over to pat Sophia's hand. "It's for the best, honey. He wasn't the man for you."

But how did Jannette know that? Just because she'd had a bad experience didn't mean all men were like Sophia's father. And Mike had so many good qualities. He was fun and optimistic. He had a positive attitude and people really liked him.

Forget him, Sophia. You're going to meet Michael today—the man you're going to marry.

How would Mike act at the picnic? she fretted. Hopefully he would be as aloof there as he had been at the office the last two weeks. She'd hate for Michael to show up and find Mike hanging around.

Sophia turned off the highway at the exit marked—Casa Del Sol Dude Ranch. A caravan of cars proceeded down the road in front of them. They arrived a few minutes later and Sophia found a parking place in the vast lot. She spotted Olivia and Lucas Hunter as they drove by, and waved.

"I can't believe Olivia came," Sophia told Jannette as she helped her from the car and into her wheelchair. "She's due to deliver that baby in just over a week."

Jannette sucked in her breath. "She should be careful! First babies are often early."

"I'm sure she'll be fine," Sophia said, but cast a worried glance over her shoulder. Lucas and Olivia were slowly making their way over.

Sophia waited on her friends, then the four of them chatted on the way to the entrance.

Lucas was so solicitous of his wife. He took her hand with one arm and gently led her across the parking area. Jealousy stabbed through Sophia. Would she ever have a man like that?

Rex Barrington and Mildred Van Hess stood at the gate, greeting everyone individually as they entered. Sophia wanted to ask him if he'd heard from his son, but she was too shy.

Hired cowboys issued a hearty welcome and herded the guests toward the activities. A large white banner with red lettering proclaimed Barrington Corporation Goodbye To Summer Picnic. Cool, blue water from a guitar-shaped pool beckoned swimmers. The corrals displayed a variety of horses for interested riders. Concession stands offered a wide selection of beverages from soft drinks to imported beers to lemonade. Numerous barbecue grills were loaded with hamburgers, hot dogs, chicken and fish. Bowls of salads, pasta and fresh fruit were laid out on trestle tables of crushed ice.

Lucas found them a long table under a brightly colored awning. He helped Olivia sit while Sophia set the parking brake on Jannette's wheelchair. Sophia then took a seat where she could watch the front entrance for Michael's appearance.

"I'll go get cold drinks," Lucas said and took their orders.

"He's such a great guy," Sophia said to Olivia with a sigh as they watched him make his way to the concession stand.

Olivia smiled demurely and wrapped her hands around her tummy. "I like to think so."

"Hello, ladies." They looked up to see Olivia's old boss, Stanley Whitcomb standing beside their table.

Olivia's face brightened. "Stanley. Sit down. You know Sophia, of course. And this is her mother, Jannette."

"Hello, Jannette." Stanley sat down next to her mother and smiled broadly. To Sophia's surprise, Jannette smiled back. Before she knew it, her mother and Stanley were deeply engrossed in conversation.

"So," Olivia whispered, "how's Mike?"

Sophia took a deep breath. "That has cooled down."

"Oh." Olivia looked disappointed. "That's a shame."

"No." Sophia shook her head. "Not really. Michael's coming to the picnic."

"Michael Barrington?"

Sophia nodded. "I'm so nervous."

"But what about Mike?"

"What about him?" Sophia asked, irritated. She wished her friend would stop bringing up the man she wanted to forget.

"What happened to cool things off?"

A very hot necking session.

"Let's not talk about Mike."

"Why not? Because you still care about him?" Olivia sent her a chiding expression.

"No."

"You don't have to lie to me."

"I'm not lying."

"Then why is Mike standing over there staring at you as if you were made of chocolate and sugar?"

"What?" Alarmed, Sophia's gaze swept the area.

Sure enough, there he was, lounging around a split-rail fence, his eyes devouring her. She did not expect her skin to catch flame, but it did. Their gazes met but she couldn't hold his stare. Her chest suddenly went tight and her head swam. She had to get away, remove herself from his propinquity before she did something rash.

Knowing she was taking a chance on missing Michael's entrance, Sophia turned to Olivia. "If my mother asks, I went to the bathroom." She glanced over to find Jannette's attention was fully focused on Stanley Whitcomb.

Head down, Sophia hustled away. Where were the rest rooms? she wondered, desperate for a cool damp towel and a place to hide out from Mike. She rounded the corner of the building and paused to catch her breath. Briefly she closed her eyes.

Calm down, Sophia, she coached herself. *You see him every day at the office. What's the big deal?*

Yes, but at the office he was fully clothed. Here, Mike wore tight blue shorts and the top three buttons on his white polo shirt were undone, revealing more of his masculine chest than she cared to see. His legs were long, tan and very muscular. Just as she had imagined they would be. And his rear end! Well, somewhere there were angels singing Hallelujah. To see her midnight fantasies brought to life like this was rather disconcerting.

"Morning, Sophia."

That voice! So warm and deep. Just like Michael Barrington's. Could it be him?

Startled, her eyes flew open and her heart dropped to her feet.

Mike.

Standing inches away. A smirk on his face, one arm draped casually against the side of the building. There was something primitive about him, something elementally male.

"Hello, Mike," she said hoarsely.

He took a step toward her and she forced herself not to slink backward, away from his heat. She could handle this.

"I've been thinking about you," he said. "A lot."

"Mike…I…"

"I can't forget what happened in your office that Friday night. Lord knows I've tried. I've kept my distance. I know I'm not what you want in a man."

Oh, but he was! He was! Therein lay the problem.

Mike was all wrong for her but Sophia wanted him. More than she could express. Her lower abdomen ached with longing whenever she looked at him. Her breast hung heavy at the remembrance of his frisky tongue. Her thighs burned with the thought of having him between them. She felt dizzy, out of control.

He reached over and gently brushed a lock of hair from her forehead. Sophia gulped against those red-hot fingertips.

"I've got something to tell you," he said huskily. The sound drove a spike of desire straight through her.

"Yes?" she whispered.

He gazed into her eyes. Sophia was shocked at what she read in those green depths.

Was Mike the mailman in love with her?

Sophia suddenly shivered. No. It couldn't be. Not a man like Mike. He could never be tied down to one woman, one city, one life.

They stood staring at each other, both enraptured by what they saw.

"What?" Sophia spoke at last. "What did you want to tell me?" Was he going to propose? What on earth would she say if he did? What would she do about Michael Barrington?

"I'm quitting my job."

Sophia stared, not sure if she'd heard him correctly.

He nodded. "I'm leaving Phoenix."

"Why?"

Mike shrugged. "I can't keep working at Barrington, caring about you the way I do, knowing you're in love with your boss, knowing there's no chance for me."

"You can't leave because of me. You like your job." She reached out to take his hand and give it a squeeze. "Please reconsider."

"There are other jobs." He gave a wry smile. "But there's no one else like you, Sophia."

No man had ever said such a wonderful thing to her. How foolish she was to let him walk away from her because he was not successful. How shallow for her to look at money as the bottom line. What mattered was how they felt about one another.

Right?

But years of Jannette's negative training contradicted that knowledge. That and Sophia's own experiences at being poor. As her mother put it, love didn't pay the rent.

"When are you leaving?" she asked.

"I'm giving my two-week notice on Monday."

"I see."

"I'll miss you."

"I'll miss you, too," she said it lightly, as if she didn't really care, but she did! She cared so much. Too much. It felt as if she'd just taken a bullet to the chest.

"I wanted you to be the first to know."

"You haven't told Mr. Barrington yet?"

"No." He lifted her hand to his lips, gently kissed her skin.

She took a breath so long and deep, it rippled through her body. "Mike?"

"Yes?"

"Kiss me."

Why was she saying this when she should be saying, "Congratulations, have a good life." She should be on her knees thanking the heavens for rescuing her from her men problems. Instead, the thought of never seeing Mike again left her feeling lonely and abandoned. If nothing else, she deserved one last kiss.

"What?"

"Kiss me."

"You mean like this?" In an instant, Mike pulled her to his chest and wrapped his arms around her.

The minute his lips grazed hers, Sophia recognized the foolishness of her request. What had she started? Why did she constantly persist in playing with fire where this man was concerned? She knew better, and yet she could not seem to help herself.

"Oh, Mike," Sophia whispered, and helplessly succumbed to his mouth.

Chapter Eight

He hadn't intended for things to play out this way.

Last night, while lying in bed thinking about Sophia, he'd promised himself he was going to tell her the truth. That he was Michael Barrington, the man she'd been scheming to marry. Instead he'd told her he was quitting Barrington Corporation and leaving town.

Why?

For this.

His mouth moved against her heated lips, soaking up her essence, reveling in the woman that was Sophia Shepherd. She intoxicated him with her clean, fresh floral scent. Her full lips drove him crazy. The smooth curve of her thigh against his leg had Mike battling to keep his arousal under control.

What he wouldn't give to slip off to the lake with Sophia and make love on the beach, their bodies sinking into the sand, the heat warming their skin, the water lapping rhythmically against the shore as they became one, in harmony with nature.

Mike felt his control slipping. Rapidly. He forgot they were at the dude ranch with hundreds of co-workers and his father and Sophia's mother in attendance. He forgot he was supposed to be proving to himself that she meant nothing to him. He forgot everything, even his own name. It didn't matter if he was Mike the mailman or Michael Barrington, corporate executive. All that mattered was Sophia. Sophia, in his arms, in his mind, in his heart.

She tasted like summer. Sultry, tempting, dangerous. Her kisses were an exotic blending of innocence and desire.

Since that night two weeks ago when they'd lost their heads in her office, Mike had been able to think of little else. And now here they were, spinning out of control again, blanketed in each other's arms.

His desperate need for so much more than kisses, finally broke through his fog of passion.

No matter how much he might wish it, he could not have her here and now. It was a public place, but much more than that, he could not make love to Sophia until she knew the truth about him. Until she accepted him for who he was, not for who she wanted him to be.

Purposefully he grasped her shoulders in both his hands and broke their kiss.

He cupped her chin in his palm, raised her face to meet his. Her blue eyes were misty with desire and it took every ounce of strength he possessed not to take those delicious lips once more.

She wanted him. He had no doubts about that. But physical lust was one thing, love was another. Could Sophia admit she loved Mike? Could she commit to a man with no future and no visible means of support? Could she let her heart lead her into his arms forever? He would not tell her he was Michael Barrington until he knew the answer to that.

"Sophia," he said simply. *Ask me to stay,* he mentally begged her. *Plead with me not to leave Phoenix.*

She smiled at him. She loved hearing him say her name. It made her feel cherished. As if she were special.

Be careful, Sophia. Cindy's words popped into her head. *It's rumored that Mike is a consummate womanizer.*

Oh, gosh, why had she practically dared him to kiss her? Had she been out of her mind? What if Michael Barrington had shown up? What if he were here now, searching the dude ranch for her?

She dropped her gaze and moved away from Mike. "I've got to get back to my mother. She'll be worried."

"All right."

"Your mind is made up? You're still going?"

His eyes clouded. "There's something else I have to tell you. Something very important."

The seriousness in his voice caught her attention. "What is it, Mike?"

"Sophia! There you are."

They looked over to see Lucas Hunter coming toward them.

"Hello, Lucas," Sophia said, anxious to relieve the tension between her and Mike. "What's up?"

"Mr. Barrington's looking for you."

"Me?" Sophia pressed a hand to herself. A heated chill zipped through her veins. Her mouth felt dry, chalky. "Wh-which Mr. Barrington?" she stammered. "Rex or Michael?"

Lucas gave her a funny look. "Why, Rex, of course. I wouldn't know Michael Barrington if he came up and tapped me on the shoulder."

On shaky legs, Sophia left the two men behind her and walked to the front entrance. People gathered in clumps. Some stood in line at the concession stand, others were at the barbecue pit, giving directions to the cook. A group of kids rode Shetland ponies in the corral.

She spotted her friends Molly and Patricia with their fiancés, Jack and Sam, lounging around the guitar-shaped swimming pool. She lifted a hand in greeting and they waved back.

Squinting against the sun and wishing she hadn't left her sunglasses on the table, Sophia scanned the crowd for a man in a white T-shirt and blue shorts. No one fit the description.

Her spirits stumbled.

Michael, where are you?

"Sophia, my dear."

She turned, saw Rex Barrington making his way through the crowd. "Hello, Mr. Barrington."

"Are you enjoying yourself?"

"Yes." She smiled. "It's a lovely party."

"I'm saddened to think it's going to be my last outing as the CEO of Barrington Corporation, but it really is time for me to retire and turn the reins over to Michael."

"Lucas said you wanted to speak to me?"

Rex nodded. "I need your help."

"My help?"

"Organizing the three-legged race."

"Oh." For some reason she had assumed Rex carried news of Michael. She hadn't expected to be drafted as race coordinator.

"All right. What do you need for me to do?"

Rex grinned and Sophia wondered if he had an ulterior motive for this race, though for the life of her she couldn't say why she'd gotten that impression.

He handed her several dozen pieces of rope about three feet long. "Tie the contestants' ankles and knees together."

Curious, she accepted the rope then watched as he

stepped up over to where a loudspeaker had been rigged up.

"May I have your attention?"

All heads turned in his direction.

"We're about to begin the three-legged race. I have selected your partners for you. As I call out your names, please assemble at the starting line on top of the hill." Mr. Barrington pointed to a rolling bluff several hundred yards away. "Sophia Shepherd will be waiting there to help you. The finish line is directly behind the concession stand. The winners will receive a free dinner at Reflections at the White Swan Hotel in Sedona."

I'm supposed to win that, Sophia thought suddenly. *Me and Michael.* Except Michael wasn't here.

While Rex laughed, joked and called out the names of the contestants and their pairings, Sophia, ropes in hand, made her way over to the bluff. Before everyone arrived, she had a brief opportunity to check the crowd again, but still no Michael. She did however, catch sight of Mike. He was sitting talking to Olivia, her mother and Mr. Whitcomb. She waved but none of them saw her.

"We're here!" Nick Delaney and Rachel Sinclair giggled.

Sophia crouched and tied Rachel's slender ankle to that of her fiancé. Then she bound them at the knees.

"Hey," Rachel asked. "I haven't had the chance to ask you how you worked things out."

"I haven't," Sophia admitted.

"Did you listen to your heart?"

"It wasn't speaking to me."

"Come now, Sophia, of course it was. You're just not listening."

"That's not too tight, is it?" Sophia asked, anxious to get Rachel off the topic.

"Perfect," Nick replied. "The closer I am to Rachel,

the better.'' He draped an arm around her shoulder and drew his bride-to-be into the circle of his arm.

They gazed into each other's eyes and grinned. Sophia felt an ugly jolt of jealousy. She wanted what those two had. Love, honesty, open communication. She wanted a committed relationship with a man she could trust. Like Rachel and Nick. Like Cindy and Kyle. Like Molly and Jack. Like Lucas and Olivia. Like Patricia and Sam. Like everyone else in the world.

An unexpected lump formed in her throat. Maybe she'd never have anyone. Was she too picky? Should she settle? Accept Mike despite his flaws? But what's to say Mike even wanted her for anything more than a good time?

Rachel and Nick hobbled off to the side, giggling and holding on to each other while another couple waited to be harnessed together.

Over the loudspeaker, she could still hear Mr. Barrington calling out the names of the contestants.

''And last, but of course not least, Mike Barr from the mail room.''

A cheer went up from the crowd. Sophia cast a glance down the hill, and watched as Mike got to his feet. Grinning boyishly, he bowed to the audience. He was very popular with the Barrington employees. She wouldn't be the only one saddened to see him leave.

''Mike is paired with Sophia Shepherd,'' Rex said.

The cheering intensified.

Sophia blushed. Great. Just what she needed. With her luck, Michael would show up at the same time she and Mike came hopping down the hill together.

''We'll have some accompanying music,'' Rex announced. Mildred Van Hess came over and put a CD into the compact disc player. A few seconds later, ''Flight of the Bumblebee'' poured from the speakers.

Mike came toward her. Sophia held two pieces of rope

in her hand. He took them from her, then bending over he clinched their ankles and knees, uniting them as one.

Raising up, he grinned at her.

"Places, everyone," Rex announced.

Laughing along with the other contestants, Sophia and Mike hobbled over to the starting line.

Why did it have to be him?

Their legs rubbed like two pieces of flint sparking a fire. Bare skin against bare skin. Sophia had never thought of ankles and knees as sexy body parts but she was quickly altering that perception.

"You know the only way we're going to sew up this race is to work as a team," Mike whispered, his breath tickling her ear.

Sophia suppressed a shudder of delight and raised a hand to her hair to block the mind-expanding sensation.

"We've got to pull together as one, going in the same direction and at the same pace."

"Who says I want to win?" Sophia crinkled her nose.

"Come on, you want to win as much as I do." His grin widened. "Let's blow them out of the water."

This side of Mike surprised her. In the nine months he'd worked at Barrington Corporation she hadn't detected one competitive bone in his body. He was usually so laid-back and devil-may-care. Why suddenly was he so interested in winning? Especially something that didn't matter? If he could be so intent about a three-legged race, why couldn't he employ the same enthusiasm toward a serious career?

These questions disturbed her. Why indeed? Mike was smart, he was likable. The only thing holding him back was his own lack of ambition. What did it take to light a fire under this man?

One kiss from me.

The thought fogged her mind like a dirty secret. No

matter how she might try to deny it or avoid it, the chemistry between them was undeniably overwhelming.

Maybe, she mused, entertaining the very notion she'd promised herself she would not fall victim to. Maybe he would change for me. Maybe chemistry would be enough to cause such a reaction in him he'd settle down and get a decent job.

Don't go there, Sophia Denise Shepherd. Don't you dare hope for it. Only Mike can change Mike.

But what if he could change? What if he were willing to change, not for her but for himself? What if he decided being a rolling stone wasn't all it was cracked up to be? What if he came to realize that home and family were the most important things in life?

The crowd had moved away from the picnic area and come to form a line along the edges of the race path. She saw Stanley Whitcomb pushing her mother's wheelchair. Olivia walked beside them. Lucas was one of the contestants, having been paired with a new employee from accounting. Jannette waved jauntily.

"Ready," Rex called out over the loudspeaker.

Mike took Sophia's hand in his. "Bend slightly at the knees," he instructed.

She obeyed, copying his stance.

"On your mark."

The contestants tensed in readiness.

"Go!"

A wild melee ensued.

Everyone rushed downhill toward the finish line.

Right away, Cindy and Kyle pulled into the lead but then Kyle stumbled and they went down. Another couple tripped over them, creating a pileup.

Mike deftly steered Sophia to one side.

They moved as one, gracefully as Olympic figure skaters. Wherever Mike led, Sophia followed. She matched his pace, neither too fast nor too slow. Their fingers remained entwined.

It was a strange ballet. And oddly erotic.

Acutely aware of his knee bobbing into hers, Sophia tried to concentrate on the race. Instead, her head was distracted by thoughts of how good they were at this. If they could make the most of being bound together, what would they be like in bed? Flesh to flesh with no cumbersome rope to impede their progress.

Sophia groaned inwardly, pushed away her fantasy and forced her thoughts back on the race. She braved a glance over at Mike and her heart stuttered. His green-eyed gaze was fixed intently on the finish line.

He wanted to win. She could see it in the set of his jaw, in the intent expression on his face. Where had this competitive spirit come from and why hadn't she seen it before? Had he purposely been keeping it under wraps? Why?

Mesmerized, Sophia neglected to watch the ground. She misstepped. Mike grabbed her elbow, attempting to correct her balance.

She flailed backward and grasped at his shirt, struggling to keep herself upright. She didn't want to cost him the race.

Her efforts proved futile. She fell.

Mike toppled over her.

They rolled together, grass and dirt hitching a ride on their clothes, in their hair.

Emotion welled inside Sophia. She'd disappointed him!

Then came the sound that surprised her.

Mike's husky laughter.

They came to a stop. Sophia's back against the ground, Mike laying atop her. The other contestants hopped past them. Sophia caught a glimpse of numerous tanned knees and scuffed sneakers. The sun shone brightly in the pristine blue sky. The air smelled of grass and Mike's cologne.

She hitched in her breath and stared up into his face.

His green eyes were filled with mirth. Smile lines bracketed his mouth. Bits of straw hung in his dark brown hair.

Gently Sophia reached up with her fingers to rake it away.

He laughed again and she could feel the vibrations bubble from deep within his chest.

They were breathing hard. In unison.

"So much for that free swanky dinner in Sedona," he said.

"Disappointed?"

"Are you?"

"I could eat a hot dog in Phoenix with you," Sophia said, startling herself. That wasn't what she'd meant to say.

"Could you, Sophia?" He spoke lightly, but the look in his eyes was deadly serious. "Could you really be happy with that?"

Yes! All she wanted was someone to share her life with. Someone she could trust. Someone who would be there for her. But was Mike that someone?

"I…"

"Lucas!" Someone shouted. Suddenly there was a loud commotion from the sidelines.

"What's going on?" Sophia asked, raising up on her elbows.

Mike rolled off her and followed her gaze.

A crowd had formed a circle around someone. Jannette? Sophia's heart leapt into her throat. She'd been so wrapped up with Mike, she had been negligent of her mother. If something had happened to her mother, Sophia would never forgive herself.

"Untie us!" she said, panicking.

"Calm down." Quickly Mike sat up and unfurled the knots in the rope. Sophia's pulse pounded.

"My mother," she said, scrambling to her feet. "What if something's happened to her?"

"Go on," Mike said. "I'm right behind you." And he was.

A sense of peace flooded over her at the knowledge that he was there. For years she had prayed and dreamed of finding a man who would stand beside her no matter what, but Sophia discovered the reality of having Mike back her up felt much better than any fantasy.

"Lucas!" Someone shouted again, and Sophia saw that someone was Jack Cavanaugh. She turned her head to spot Lucas and his partner at the finish line. They had won the race.

"Olivia's in labor," Jack shouted, cupping his hands around his mouth to be heard above the din.

That explained the crowd. Relieved to know her mother was okay, but concerned about her friend, Sophia rushed over.

Olivia was sitting in a folding chair holding her abdomen and trying to be brave. Lucas arrived seconds after Sophia. He pushed everyone aside, scooped his wife into his arms and carried her across the field.

A procession consisting of Olivia and Lucas's friends fell in behind them.

"I can walk, Lucas!" Olivia insisted.

"The hell you say," Lucas growled.

The crowd chuckled.

Mike took Sophia's arm. "I'm betting you'd be just as stubborn as Olivia."

"And you'd be as opinionated as Lucas."

He suppressed a grin.

"Sophia."

She let go of Mike's hand and went over to speak to

her mother who was being wheeled along by Stanley Whitcomb.

"Hi, Mom." Sophia leaned over to kiss Jannette on the cheek. "Having a good time?"

"Yes." Jannette smiled shyly. Sophia was pleased and surprised to see her mother looking so happy.

"Sophia, if you'd like to go on to the hospital with Olivia and Lucas, I'd be happy to give your mother a ride home," Stanley Whitcomb interjected.

"That's so nice of you to offer," Sophia said, "but we couldn't impose."

"No imposition at all," Stanley said.

"But the wheelchair..."

"I drive a sport utility vehicle. I have plenty of room," Stanley assured her.

"Mom?"

"Run along." Jannette made shooing motions with her hands. "I know you're dying to go."

"You don't mind?" It seemed so odd, seeing her mother happy in the company of a man. In all the twenty-nine years that Sophia had known her, Jannette had never dated. This new turn of events perplexed her.

Jannette shook her head. "Go."

"All right, then." Feeling like a mother leaving her child alone on the first day of school, Sophia followed Mike to the parking lot.

"You want to ride with me to the hospital?" she quizzed.

Mike melted her with his grin. "I thought you'd never ask."

He wandered the halls of the hospital, feeling at loose ends. Sophia sat in the waiting room with her friends chatting gaily about babies. The other guys had gone off to look at Nick's new truck but Mike had stayed behind. He had too many things to think about.

Mainly, how to tell Sophia the truth.

Each encounter, each touch, each smile, each kiss brought them one step closer to…what?

Commitment?

But how could they commit when he wasn't being honest with her? And what about her determination to marry a rich man? Where did that leave him but back at square one?·

The truth was, he liked being Mike. He liked not having the responsibilities. He liked having friends whose motives he did not have to question. He liked feeling footloose and fancy-free, even if it was only an illusion. It had been eye-opening, these past nine months, exploring a side of himself he thought long dead. From the time he could walk, he'd wanted nothing more than to follow in Rex's footsteps. He'd learned all he could about the hotel business. He'd studied hard, learned the inner workings of the company from the inside out. He never took vacations. He worked fourteen-hour days. He had made Barrington Corporation his life.

It had been nice, for a while to play the irresponsible bad boy. The experience of assuming someone else's skin had taught him a lot about stopping and smelling the roses before life passed him by. Mike the mailman might not be rich, but he was a much happier man than Rex Michael Barrington III.

Deep in thought, Mike stuffed his hands in his back pockets. He stopped outside the waiting room and peered in the glass window.

The room was soundproof. He couldn't hear what they were saying, but he could tell Sophia was laughing at something Cindy had said. Her eyes crinkled at the corners, her lips turned up just the way he liked them. The men had come back from the parking lot and had taken their places beside their women. Cindy and Kyle. Molly and Jack. Nick and Rachel. Patricia and Sam. They all belonged together. They formed a tight friendship. A close-knit group of Barrington employees.

A group that Michael Barrington could never be part of. He was the mysterious voice on the telephone. Their boss. The rich guy. He didn't fit in.

On the outside looking in. Mike swallowed hard. As he had been all his life. Until now, he'd used hard work and self-sacrifice to assuage his loneliness. The loneliness that had been a big part of his life for thirty-six years. He'd denied that he needed or even wanted anything more than his career. Now he knew how much more there was to life. He wanted what his employees had found. True and lasting love.

Sophia lifted her head. Their gazes locked. Her smile widened, encompassing him in a warm glow. She got to her feet and walked toward the door.

Her easy grace, the sway of her hips, that look in her eyes. Mike's knees went weak.

He loved her.

No matter how hard he might want to pretend that she had not invaded his heart, had not seized his soul, it was a lie. She had captured him. Completely.

Except he was not the man *she* believed him to be. He was not the man she wanted.

"Hi." Sophia popped out into the hallway, her hands crossed over her chest. "Have a nice walk?"

"I get jittery if I sit long."

She nodded. "Hospitals are nerve-wracking places."

Mike knew that. How many long, ugly hours had he spent in this very hospital, watching his mother slowly fade away while he was helpless to intervene? All the Barrington money in the whole world had not been able to save her.

Couldn't Sophia see that? Didn't she realize that money could not buy life or happiness or freedom? Money was a tool and nothing more. It wasn't a god to be worshiped or something to cling to. Money could not hold you tight in the middle of the night when you woke from a bad dream. Money could not stop the spread of cancer. Nor could it bring real friends into the life of a lonely boy.

"Want to grab some coffee?" she invited.

"Sure." Mike shrugged and walked with her down the hall to the cafeteria. He felt awkward with her. He didn't know what to do. His plan to make her fall in love with Mike the mailman had backfired, failing miserably.

He fed coins into the coffee vending machine, then punched the buttons. He knew how Sophia liked hers. With lots of milk and sugar. They took their cups and went to sit at a table near the window.

"I'm so nervous for Lucas and Olivia. I hope things go okay."

"They'll be fine. They love each other, those two. No matter what happens, they'll make it."

"Yeah," Sophia said wistfully and stared out the window deep in thought.

Was she, like he, thinking about true love, happy marriages and healthy babies? Did she feel the same internal longings he felt?

"Are you serious about leaving Phoenix?" she asked.

"I've got no reason to stay, Sophia."

"Oh." Her bottom lip quivered.

Mike toyed with the napkin holder on the table, unable to meet Sophia's stare. He wanted so badly to tell her the truth but he didn't know how to start.

"Can I ask you a question?" she ventured.

"Shoot." He cradled his coffee cup in his palms.

"Do you ever see yourself settling down, committing to one town, one job, one woman?"

Yes! How he longed to tell her what was really in his heart. But he couldn't. This was the perfect opportunity to find out for sure. Would she accept Mike the mailman for exactly who he was? Would she relinquish her infatuation with her boss and announce her love for Mike?

"Sophia, Mike!" Molly burst through the door, her face flushed. "The nurse told us it's a boy!"

Sophia jumped to her feet and embraced Molly. They jumped about the room, excited as children at Christmas.

"Come on, come on." Molly motioned them to hurry. "Lucas is coming out any minute to give us the details."

They trooped back to the waiting room just in time to see Lucas grinning from ear to ear. "It's a miracle," he kept saying over and over. "I can't explain how wonderful it feels."

For a moment Lucas was so overcome with emotion that he could not speak. "There's nothing in the world like it."

The four other couples all turned to each other, clasped hands and smiled as if they couldn't wait for their own miracles.

Mike cast a sideways glance at Sophia. She had her hands clasped together in front of her and her lips were pressed into a firm line as if she were trying not to cry. His heart ached for her. He longed to reach out and touch her. To tell her he understood the depths of her feelings. But he could not.

"Come on, everyone," Lucas said, "let's go see my son."

Talking excitedly, they descended upon the nursery. Lucas beamed proudly as a nurse held his wriggling baby boy up to the nursery window for all to see.

"May I present to you Nathaniel Wyatt Hunter. Eight pounds, six ounces with an excellent set of lungs."

Everyone chuckled and gathered closer for a better look at the newest arrival. The ladies oohed and aahed over the infant while the men slapped Lucas playfully on the back.

"Good work, Hunter," Jack said.

"You gotta be proud." Nick grinned.

"He's a fine-looking boy," Sam contributed.

"Bet he's going to give you and Olivia a run for your money," Kyle added.

"Your life will never be the same," Mike said. "Your bachelor days are gone for good."

Sophia jerked her head to stare at Mike. Was that how he saw fatherhood? As an end, not a wondrous beginning? But what else could she expect from a man who could not stay put in one place long enough to develop a relationship?

"No," Lucas said. "You've got it all wrong, Mike. With Nathaniel and Olivia, my life has just begun." He smiled affectionately at his son through the nursery window.

Sadness streaked through Sophia. How could she have lost her head over a man like Mike? Despite her best efforts to the contrary, despite trying to make herself fall in love with Michael Barrington, she had tumbled into that same sorrowful trap that had once snared her mother. She had foolishly allowed herself to be swept away by chemistry.

Unable to face him, knowing how he felt about babies and marriage and permanence of any kind, Sophia took Nick aside and asked him to give Mike a ride home. Then without a word of explanation, she disappeared, anxious to get as far away from this hospital and the happy event as she could.

It was only much later, as she was lying alone in bed that night, that Sophia realized Michael Barrington had never shown up at the company picnic.

Chapter Nine

"Sophia." Michael Barrington's voice poured out of the receiver like rich Colombian coffee. "I've got to apologize for standing you up this weekend. I tried to make it back to Phoenix in time for the picnic, I truly did, but something unexpected came up. Looks like I'm going to be in Germany several more days."

Sophia stared listlessly at the wall. Olivia had been correct. Michael Barrington was too busy for a relationship. He stood people up and then expected work to be a viable excuse with no questions asked. She'd been foolish to think she could ever marry a man like him. They came from two different worlds. They had absolutely nothing in common.

"Don't worry about it, sir. I understand completely. You're a very busy man and business comes first."

"Hey, what's this? I thought we agreed, no more 'sir.' You're supposed to call me Michael," he chided her.

"I've been thinking about it and I don't think it sounds very professional."

"Since when?"

Since you made promises you don't keep. Since I real-ized I'm not in love with you.

"All right, Sophia," he replied quietly. "Whatever you wish."

He told her goodbye and hung up, leaving her feeling cold and empty inside. She sure had a penchant for picking unavailable men. On the one hand there was Michael—accomplished, successful, stable and financially secure, but he was an emotionally distant workaholic. On the other hand there was Mike—fun-loving, exciting, sexy and very handsome but utterly unable to commit to a job, a woman or even to a city.

"Knock, knock." Patricia Peel appeared in her door-way. "How are you this morning?"

"Hi, Patricia," Sophia greeted the assistant personnel director. "Come on in."

"How about that picnic?" Patricia said, strolling into Sophia's office. "Was the birth of Olivia's baby the grand finale or what?"

"It did add fireworks to the proceedings. Hey, want to see the baby blanket I bought Olivia when I went shopping on my lunch hour?" Sophia pulled a sack from beneath her desk and unwrapped the blue quilt decorated with teddy bears and trains.

"That's so darling," Patricia cooed. "Olivia's so lucky."

Sophia nodded and sighed in spite of herself. Patricia mistook her sigh for one of hopeful longing rather than for what it really was—despair.

"I know." Patricia smiled. "I'm so jealous. I can't wait to marry Sam and start having babies of our own."

"When's the wedding?"

"Not until June." Patricia groaned. "It seems ages away."

"It'll be here before you know it." Sophia placated her friend. She didn't want to talk about weddings or babies or happiness. It simply wasn't fair!

All her friends were in love. They had found good men and were in the process of getting married or starting their families. Why had she been left out? Why was she the only one without someone to love her? Even her mother had struck up a budding relationship with Stanley Whitcomb. And as happy as Sophia was for Jannette, she couldn't help but feel a little sorry for herself.

Sophia pushed her hands through her hair. Her life was falling apart. All the plans she'd made were nothing but hollow pipe dreams. A lump formed in her throat, but Sophia swallowed it back. She wasn't the type to wallow in self-pity. If God intended for her to be alone the rest of her life, then so be it. She'd find some way to fill the long, lonely years stretching before her.

"I thought you might want to know," Patricia said. "Mike turned in his resignation today."

Patricia's words hit her like a punch. Sophia sucked in her breath. So he'd gone through with it. She'd only thought her spirits were low before. That bit of news served to send her lingering hopes spinning into outer space.

"Oh?" she said, trying to act coolly disinterested while inside her tummy burned.

"Didn't he tell you?"

Sophia shrugged, feigning indifference. "He might have mentioned something about it."

"You're not upset?"

"Why on earth should I be upset?" Sophia struggled to keep her hand from trembling. She didn't care. Good riddance. Who needed passion, heat and chemistry? Who needed their world turned upside down and inside out? Certainly not she.

"Well—" Patricia looked hesitant "—I sort of assumed you two were an item."

Sophia laughed but it sounded forced even to her own ears. "Whatever gave you that idea?"

"You two seemed to get along so well together. I don't know. You made a cute couple."

"We were never a couple," Sophia denied hotly.

Patricia raised both her palms. "Sorry. My mistake. Mike was just so popular around the office that we're all going to miss him."

"Don't get me wrong," Sophia said. "I'm fond of Mike. He's a fun guy. But he means nothing to me personally. Absolutely nothing."

Her voice cracked.

"You're in love with him, aren't you?" Patricia said seriously.

Silently Sophia nodded. Fat tears unexpectedly slipped down her cheeks.

"Oh, sweetie." Patricia came around the desk to wrap her arms around Sophia. "It'll all work out."

"How can it? Mike's leaving. And even if he wasn't, he's not the kind of guy you build a future with."

Patricia handed her a tissue. "It might not work out with Mike, but you'll find someone. I promise you."

"Really?" Sophia dabbed at her eyes.

"Cross my heart."

"A guy I can depend on? Someone who'll be a good husband. A man who'll stand by me through thick and thin, no matter what?"

"If you refuse to settle for less."

"That's a tall order to fill."

"Hey," Patricia said, snapping her fingers. "What about Michael Barrington? I thought you were hoping to date him when he came home to take over the business?"

"That was just a silly infatuation. I've learned a few things since then."

"Oh?"

"Yes. Work means more to Michael Barrington than any woman ever could. I don't want to play second fiddle to anyone's career."

"I suppose it's better to learn that now, before you ever got involved with him."

Sophia nodded. It sounded so sensible coming from her friend, but in the course of a single morning she'd lost both of the men she'd been interested in. It hurt. Here she was, twenty-nine and baby hungry with no marriage prospects in sight.

"Cheer up, Sophia, and mark my words. One of these days you'll find your Prince Charming."

Yeah? When I'm ninety-five?

"Thanks," Sophia said, resolutely tucking the tissue in her pocket. "You've been a big help."

And it was true. Her friend's sympathy went a long way to ease the sorrow weighing down her heart. Everyone at the Barrington Corporation had been great. In the two years she had worked here Sophia had come to feel like part of the family. And for a little girl who'd once been shunned and outcast because of a background she couldn't help, that meant a lot.

"You're welcome." Patricia smiled. "Oh, I almost forgot. Olivia asked me if you could type up the contract on the Helsberg account. Stanley's new assistant hasn't quite gotten the hang of things and Olivia knew you were familiar with the details."

"Sure," Sophia readily agreed. Anything to help her friend. She'd have to stay late, after she got her own work done, but that was all right. She needed something to keep her mind off Mike.

"You're a doll. And remember, chin up."

Sophia smiled and waved goodbye but beneath the facade her heart was breaking.

"You haven't told Sophia yet?" Rex Barrington frowned at his only son.

They were having an early supper at a hotel Rex was considering acquiring on the shores of Lake Olivet in the resort community of Briarton, located twenty-six miles southwest of Phoenix. He'd wanted Michael's opinion before closing the deal.

The place was pretty, Michael conceded. Another feather in the Barrington cap. But right now he didn't really care. The setting sun was spectacular, but he scarcely noticed the vivid burst of salmon, purple and rose streaking the sky. A band played soft music. Sailboats glided across the water in front of the shaded veranda where they sat dining on shrimp cocktail and grilled flounder. Except he wasn't hungry and his plate remained untouched.

"No," Michael admitted, taking a sip of his Scotch and water. "I haven't talked to her."

He'd meant to tell Sophia who he really was. A dozen times or more. But something had always stopped him. The time had never been right. But then again, was there ever an appropriate time to tell the woman you loved that you were a liar and a fraud and a fake?

Rex cleared his throat. "You're not being fair to her."

"I know, Dad, but it's just not that simple."

"She's in love with you, Michael. Can't you see that?"

"She's not in love with me. She's in love with an image, a part I've been playing."

"Isn't that what you wanted? To trick her into falling in love with a poor man so you'd know for sure she wasn't after your money?"

"Yes. No. I don't know."

Frustrated, Michael stared out across the water. He

didn't know what to believe anymore. Once upon a time the Barrington Corporation was the most important thing in his world. He'd lived and breathed the business. He'd only wanted to make his father proud by expanding the company, earning more money, making things bigger and better. Suddenly, something had Michael questioning all his old values.

And that something was Sophia Shepherd.

He could not, no matter how hard he tried, erase her from his mind. That blond hair, so long and curly, dominated his dreams. Her scent, like fresh wildflowers, teased his nostrils at the most unexpected times. Her lips, so soft, so pliant, branded his memory and refused to dissipate.

Sweet, petite Sophia. With a heart of platinum and a will of steel. She knew what she wanted and she'd been unable to settle for less. How could he blame her? Wasn't he built like that, too?

He passed judgment on her for letting her mother run her life, but hadn't he done the very same thing when at his mother's dying behest, he'd turned his back on his carefree, fun-loving nature to cultivate his serious side? When he'd tamed down the part of him that was wild and creative in favor of his button-down life?

Michael had criticized Sophia for seeking financial security, but didn't he do it on a daily basis? He made deals. He toyed with the stock market. He kept an eye on the bottom line. His whole life was about money but then he had the audacity to be resentful when people admired him for his ability to produce it. If anyone had ever sent out mixed signals, it was Rex Michael Barrington III.

Truthfully, he'd never been able to reconcile the dual aspects of his nature. When Michael had promised his mother he would leave his errant youth behind, he'd meant it. In order to deal with his inner conflict, he had buried that part of himself that was the epitome of Mike the mailman. By constantly focusing on work and leaving no room for anything else in his world.

He'd paid a high price.

Other than his father, he had no one he could truly trust. No one to rely on. No one he could reveal himself to.

But he wanted that. So badly. Those moments at the hospital when Lucas and Olivia's baby had been born had shown Michael what he'd been missing. Love. Hope. Joy.

He wanted Sophia.

The first step to achieving his goal was to find her and tell her the truth. That he was both Michael and Mike. He was at once serious and carefree, wealthy and poor, stable yet risky. He was all these things and more.

Could Sophia accept him? Would she take him just as he was? Most importantly, did she love him enough to forgive his deceit?

There was only one way to find out.

Michael pushed back his chair and stood up. He pulled a handful of bills from his wallet and left them on the table.

"Buy the hotel if you want," he told his father. "I've got unfinished business to take care of in Phoenix."

It was almost seven o'clock when Sophia finished typing up the Helsberg contract. She'd called Olivia at home to let her know it had been completed. After discussing baby Nathaniel and the joys of new motherhood for several minutes, Olivia had asked Sophia to make sure the contract got to the mail room before she left the office so it would go out in the morning mail.

"No problem," Sophia had said. Then it occurred to her she was going to have to go down into the basement. After hours. Alone.

She hated the thought of running into Mike. Especially since she'd so successfully avoided him all day, planning to be out of the office when she knew he usually made his mail runs.

Don't worry. Mike will have gone home hours ago, she reassured herself. *In fact, he's probably out riding his Harley in the desert right about now.*

Why did she have such a sudden urge to be out there riding with him, the wind rushing through her hair, the setting sun in the distance, her arms wrapped tightly around Mike's warm body.

Stop it! Get your purse and Nathaniel's baby quilt, get the contract, go down to the mail room, push the envelope through the mail slot and head for home. Forget about Mike!

Except she could not. Everything reminded her of him. The glass cat paperweight prominently displayed on her desk, the length of rope that had bound them together during the three-legged race draped across her lamp, the number of the pizza delivery service on the telephone speed dial where Mike had programmed it in.

Agitated with herself, Sophia sealed a large manila envelope with the Helsberg contract inside, and addressed it to the office in Germany. She shouldered her purse, tucked the sack with the baby quilt under her arm, shut out the lights and locked her door. She walked through the empty corridor. The only sound she heard was a janitor running the vacuum cleaner somewhere down the hall.

She got on the elevator and pressed the button for the basement. She watched the numbers light up as the car descended, her chest curiously growing tighter with each passing floor.

It settled on the basement floor with a *ding*.

The door slid open.

Sophia stepped out into the darkened hallway and hurried over to the mail slot in the door. She slide the envelope inside then turned to go back to the elevator.

"What are you doing here?"

Terrified, Sophia clutched her chest with her right hand and accidentally dropped Nathaniel's baby quilt. Wide-eyed, she looked up to see Mike emerging from a side door, a key ring in his hand.

"I'm sorry," he apologized. "I didn't mean to scare you."

Oh, no! What was Mike doing here at this time of night? He was the last person she wanted to see.

"You didn't," she lied. She would not let him know exactly how much he affected her.

He sauntered toward her, his boots echoing against the tile.

The fluorescent hallway lights flickered off, then buzzed back on. Startled, Sophia gasped.

"Don't worry," Mike said. "I'm sure Rex paid the electricity bill. Must have been a power surge."

"Of course," she replied, feeling foolish.

Mike bent over and picked up the baby quilt. With fingers that felt as numb as frozen sausages, Sophia accepted the sack from him.

"Thank you," she whispered, unable to look him in the eyes.

He moved to the elevator and pressed the up button.

"Working late again?"

She nodded.

"I wonder if Michael Barrington fully appreciates everything you do for him."

"I was helping out Olivia," she explained.

"Oh."

The elevator door opened. Mike stepped inside.

Sophia hesitated. Did she really want to get into that elevator with him? In that tiny little box where they would be separated by no more than a few feet.

"Going up?" He grinned, quirked an eyebrow and cocked his head sideways.

What the heck? she thought. It's only one floor.

Bravely Sophia thrust back her shoulders and stepped over the threshold. Mike stood on the left side of the elevator, near the control panel, his finger on the Open Door button.

Sophia moved to the right rear of the car and pressed her back firmly against the wall in order to support her wobbly knees. She clutched the baby quilt to her chest and found herself staring straight ahead while waiting for the elevator door to close.

It seemed to take hours.

She knew Mike was looking at her, the heat from his gaze palpable, but she didn't have the courage to look back.

The tension stretched like a steel ribbon between them. Taut and unmistakable.

Finally the door whispered shut and the elevator started upward.

Mike cleared his throat.

Sophia studied her shoes, noticed they needed polishing.

"I suppose you heard I turned in my resignation today."

"Yes."

"How do you feel about that?"

She flashed him a look. "How do you expect me to feel?"

"I was hoping you'd miss me."

"Why should I?"

A puzzled expression crossed his face. "I thought we had something going on, you and I."

"Yeah? If that's true, how come you're leaving town?"

He jutted his chin forward. "To give you free access to Michael Barrington. I don't want to crowd you."

"Bull!" she said vehemently. "That's just an excuse."

"Now wait a minute." He raised his palms. "You made it perfectly clear you couldn't become involved with me because you had a thing for your boss. What was I supposed to do?"

"Quit. Run away," Sophia jeered. "That's your M.O., isn't it, Mike? Never too long in the same town or on the same job or with the same woman."

"Doublespeak, Sophia. You say one thing but mean another. How am I supposed to stay and fight for you when you made it abundantly clear I'm not good enough for you?"

"I never said that," she denied, ire sparking in her eyes as she glared at him. He was so damned handsome and so spectacularly sexy looking in those faded jeans and that form-fitting T-shirt. "You're good enough for me."

"But not rich enough, right?"

"Be fair. This isn't about money."

"Then what's it about?"

"It's about having a man I can count on." Sophia spoke softly. "A man whom I can trust to be there in the tough times. An honest man who won't lie to me or make excuses for his behavior. A man who will assume responsibility for his family by holding down a decent job."

"And you don't think I can be that man?" He sank his hands on his hips.

"No, I don't."

"But Michael Barrington fits the bill, and it doesn't hurt that he's a multimillionaire," Mike challenged. "Does it?"

"This isn't about Michael Barrington. This is about you and me," Sophia said.

Suddenly the elevator jerked. The cables whined, echoing loudly in the elevator shaft as the car ground to a halt.

"What was that?" she asked.

"I'm not sure."

They both glanced up at the lights over the door. First floor.

But the door did not slide open.

"Mike?" Sophia hated that her voice trembled, but she was a tad claustrophobic. "Why isn't the door opening?"

"Minor glitch. Nothing to worry about." He leaned over and mashed the Open Door button.

Nothing happened.

Sophia took a deep breath to steady herself while Mike tried the button again. "I get nervous in small, confined places," she confessed.

"I'll get us out of here," he reassured her. He started pressing all the buttons. "Stay calm, sweetheart."

Sweetheart.

That one word went a long way in allaying her anxieties.

The elevator still refused to respond.

They heard a clanking noise, like something mechanical malfunctioning. Mike frowned. "What the heck?" he said, and then the lights went out. Darkness closed around them like a gloved fist.

"Mike!" Sophia squeaked.

"Right here, sweetheart."

His hand groped for hers. She gave him her palm and he squeezed. "Don't worry. I'm here. You're not alone."

No, she was not alone. Instead, she was trapped in the darkness with the one man in the world who stirred her soul and set her body aflame. A man she loved so desperately yet could never claim as her own!

Chapter Ten

"Are you all right?" Mike asked, his fingers now entwined with Sophia's. It was odd to feel him but not be able to see his features.

"Yes."

"You wouldn't happen to have a flashlight or matches in your purse, would you?"

"I'm sorry, no."

"It's okay."

"What do you think happened?"

"Power failure of some kind."

Under the anonymity of darkness, his voice sounded exactly like Michael Barrington's. It oozed a warm sensuality that surprised Sophia in its likeness to her boss's whiskey-smooth tones.

"I'm going to fumble around over here, see if I can find the phone and call for help. Will you be all right?" he asked.

Sophia nodded then realized how ridiculous that was. He could not see her. "I'll be fine," she said, fighting panic at the thought of losing contact with him.

"Are you scared?"

"A little."

"Don't be." He let go of her hand and the air around her moved as Mike inched his way over to the front of the elevator. She kept her fingers curled around the sack holding the baby quilt, taking comfort in the softness of the material. The sack made a crinkling noise that sounded irrationally loud.

"Any luck?" Sophia asked him, anxious to fill the unnerving silence and calm her fears.

"It's like swimming through cream soup. I can't see a thing."

Sophia heard Mike running his hand along the wall. "Ouch," he exclaimed.

"What happened?"

"Jammed my thumb on the emergency button."

"I'm sorry."

"Not your fault."

There were more fumbling noises. Then the sound of a telephone being knocked off the hook and the familiar dial tone filled the car with a resounding loudness.

"Hello?" Mike spoke.

Sophia huddled against the back of the car, waiting. Already it was growing warmer and the air seemed stale.

"Hello, Operator?"

"Did you get someone?" Sophia whispered.

"Not yet."

"Hello? Yes."

Someone had answered! Sophia exhaled and it was only then that she realized she'd been holding her breath. She listened while Mike explained their situation to whoever was on the other end of the line. He muttered a few words of concern then a few seconds later, hung up.

"Well?" Sophia asked.

"There was a major accident on the freeway. An eighteen-wheeler ran into a transformer, knocking out the power in a twenty-block area. They're sending someone after us but apparently we're not real high on the priority list. They have several other emergencies.''

"What does that mean?"

"We may be stuck here for hours."

Stuck? Here? In the elevator car? Alone? With Mike?

Sophia gulped and closed her eyes against the myriad of emotions rushing through her. Excitement, trepidation, nervousness, longing, anticipation.

"Maybe the power outage is a sign from God," Mike said, his voice teasing.

"A sign from God?" Sophia repeated.

"We've had the hardest time getting together for a serious talk. Maybe this is His way of intervening."

"Oh."

"There's something I've been trying to tell you for weeks now, Sophia, and it's not going to be easy."

Alarm raced through her at his words. The worse had already happened. He was leaving Phoenix with her heart in his hands. What else could he have to say that would change that?

"Maybe you shouldn't bare your soul to me," she said. "What would be the point?"

"We might as well sit down," Mike said. "It's going to be a long night."

"Mom's going to be worried," Sophia said. "Do you think I can call her?"

"The phone's only for emergencies," Mike said. "It's not connected to an outside line."

"Oh, dear." She felt him drawing closer to her.

"I'm sure someone will contact your mother when word gets out we're trapped in here."

"We could unwrap the baby quilt and sit on that," Sophia said. "It will be more comfortable than the floor, and

I'm sure Olivia will understand.'' In the darkness, her fingers stripped the sack from the quilt. She leaned down to spread the quilt on the floor. ''There, now.''

Mike sank down, reached out, grabbed her wrist and pulled her down beside him. Sophia had never seen such complete and utter blackness. No light of any kind bled into the car. It was as if they were suspended in an endless tunnel where nothing existed except the two of them.

Mike slipped his arm around her shoulder and eased her to him. ''Do you mind?'' he whispered.

Mind! Oh, heavens no. She leaned into him, pressed her ear to his chest and listened to the steady, comfortable lubdub of his heart.

His stomach growled and Sophia giggled. ''You're hungry.''

''Didn't eat supper.''

''Me, either.''

''Too bad we don't have that pizza we ordered that evening a few weeks ago and never got around to eating,'' Mike said.

Heat rose in her cheeks as Sophia remembered exactly what had taken their attention off the pizza.

''I've got cheese and crackers in my purse,'' she volunteered, groping in the darkness for the handbag she'd laid down along with the paper sack. She blindly searched the interior until her fingers grazed across the cellophane package.

''You must have been a Girl Scout,'' Mike teased. ''You're always prepared.''

''No,'' Sophia denied. ''No Girl Scouts for me.''

''Why not?''

''Mom couldn't afford it, but I always wanted to join.''

Sophia peeled open the package, passed him a cracker and then took one for herself. She munched on the cracker, amazed at how good it tasted, with its tangy cheese flavor, the salty texture. The black void stretched into nothingness, sharpening her senses. Sounds were more intense, smells sharper. For the first time, Sophia detected the scent of oranges in Mike's cologne. Was this what it was like to be blind? she wondered. All your other senses so attuned, so aware of every nuance.

"You were really poor growing up, weren't you?"

"Yes."

"It must have been hard for you," he said a few minutes later.

Sophia snorted. "You don't know the half of it."

"No," he said. "I don't."

"What was your childhood like?" she asked. "Do you have a mother? A father? Where did you grow up?"

Maybe, Mike thought this was the perfect entry into what he had to tell her. Brushing cracker crumbs from his fingers, he then pulled her closer. It felt great to have her snuggled against him. The inky darkness seemed to ease his confession. He pressed his nose to her head, inhaled the sweet scent of her hair. Heaven!

"My mother's no longer living," he said. "She died of breast cancer fifteen years ago."

"Oh, Mike. I'm sorry."

"She was a truly wonderful woman."

"My mother had a stroke when I was eighteen. I know what's it like to have a family member who's seriously ill."

"Yeah," he said huskily. "It's rough."

"What about your father?" she asked.

"He's fine."

"Where does he live?"

The time had come to tell her the truth. But not just yet. First, he had to know that she would commit to him as Mike. Once she'd passed his test and he knew he could trust her, then he'd reveal himself. But he was not going to outright lie to her. Not anymore.

"My father lives here in Phoenix."

"Really?"

"Yes."

"Why didn't you tell me that Phoenix was your home?"

He had to change the subject, before she delved deeper into his past. "What about your father?"

Sophia tensed. Mike felt her muscles contract as she shifted away from him. "My father was a liar and a cheat." Her tone was bitter.

"How so?"

"He told my mother that he loved her. That he wanted to marry her. But he was lying just to get her into bed. Mom was only seventeen and so much in love, she couldn't think straight."

"And she got pregnant."

"Yeah," Sophia whispered.

Mike said nothing. The pain in her voice was sharp and fresh. Clearly she'd never forgiven the man.

"When Mom told him, my father demanded she have an illegal abortion. He didn't want me or my mother. But she refused to abort me. Later she found out my father was already married. Can you believe that?"

"Unfortunately it's not an uncommon story. Your mother must have had a very difficult time."

"Terrible. Her parents were ashamed. They sent her away to live with Aunt Sophia in a small town outside Phoenix. They wanted her to give me up for adoption, but Mom refused. I was all she had."

Suddenly a lot of things made sense. Jannette's anger toward men. Sophia's devotion to her mother. Sophia's need to marry a man who could take care of her. Mike felt sympathy for Jannette's desperation. She'd filled her daughter's head with horror stories in order to keep Sophia from following in her footsteps. She'd only wanted the best in life for her daughter. Something she'd never had. She thought a rich man could supply those things for her.

"What happened to your father?" Mike asked. "Did you ever hear from him again?"

"Thankfully, no. He was sent to Vietnam and killed in the war." Sophia shuddered and Mike could tell she was crying. Gently he pulled her close to him again.

"Shhh, it's all right."

"No," she denied. "It's not all right. Because of him my mother was never happy. She was scared to trust men again. She never even tried to date. Her resentment grew and she developed high blood pressure which eventually caused her stroke."

Mike reached up with his thumbs and brushed the wet tears from her cheeks. Her skin was so soft beneath his fingertips. He battled the urge to take her lips with his, to drink her nectar.

No, his inner voice cautioned. Not yet. Not until they'd cleared the air and set the record straight.

"My father's abandonment affected me, too," Sophia admitted. "The way I think about men."

"I know."

She drew in a heavy sigh. "I thought all I had to do was find a nice man with a good job. One who could support me. One who would never lie to me or take advantage of me."

Mike said nothing, simply allowed her to talk. This had been a long time coming, and obviously this emotional catharsis was something she needed.

"See," she said, "when Mom met my dad, they had this instant chemical reaction." She snapped her fingers. "Fireworks."

"Like us."

"Yes."

"And you were afraid because we have such a strong connection that I was like your dad?" Mike asked.

"I know it sounds crazy, but after listening to years of warning from my mother, I saw sexual attraction as a bad thing. I told myself my relationships would be calm and safe, based on mutual interests and honesty, not on some explosive physical reaction."

"That explains a lot about you."

"You changed everything," she said.

"I did?"

"The way I feel when I'm with you is unbelievable," Sophia confessed.

Mike groped for both her hands, brought them to his lips and kissed her knuckles one by one. "I feel it, too, sweetheart."

"Do you? Do you really?"

"You can't tell?"

"You wouldn't lie to me, would you, Mike? I couldn't bear it if I found out you'd lied to me."

"Oh, Sophia."

He had lied to her! How could he explain his charade, the way he'd allowed her to believe he was nothing more than the charming man from the mail room?

"Where are you going when you leave Phoenix?" she asked. "Will you come back to visit your father?"

"I don't have to leave," he said, feeling the quicksand of falsehoods dragging him deeper into the tangled web he'd woven for himself. "I could stay."

"What are you saying, Mike? That we could have a future together, you and I?" Sophia's heart thudded hopefully. Could it be true? The possibility swelled inside her. At long last a man to love?

"I want you, Sophia, more than I've ever wanted any woman." Mike tucked her into the circle of his arms, pressed his forehead against hers. The bond between them was a physical thing—strong, unbreakable.

Sophia reached out and ran her palm along his jawline. She caressed his dear face, enjoyed the sensation of his beard stubble rasping against her skin.

"Dear Mike, can you stop your roaming for me? Can you give up your carefree life-style and commit to our relationship? I have to know. Do your feelings for me run deep enough for you to change your lifestyle?"

"What if I said yes, Sophia? What if I told you I was already tired of wandering long before I met you and one taste of your sweet lips had thoroughly convinced me that there was no other woman on the face of the earth for me?"

"Do you mean it?" She gasped sharply.

"Would you give up your dream of marrying your boss? Or do I have to be wealthy in order to win your love?"

"Mike, I never wanted money."

And that was true! Riches had been Jannette's dream for her future. All Sophia had ever wanted was someone she could count on to be there for her. She wanted what all her friends had found—true and lasting love. Hot, sizzling chemistry was a terrific side benefit, but what Sophia sorely needed from a man was a life partner who would cherish her in good times and as well as in bad.

"Be honest with me, Sophia. If it's Michael Barrington you want, then have the guts to tell me. If it's money you seek, let me know."

"I am being honest with you, Mike. I need a husband who has a steady job. I need a man I can lean on. But I don't need a fancy car and chic clothes. I don't need jewelry and a big house or lavish trips to make me happy. Actually, working for Michael Barrington has taught me that lesson more than anything else could have."

"What about those doodles on your notepad? What

about the things you told Olivia?'' The tone of his voice changed, became harder.

Sophia frowned. Had she said something wrong? "I thought I wanted to marry Michael because he was kind to me.''

"That's it? You were going to base a marriage on kindness?''

"Among other things.''

"Like what?''

"Mom would have been pleased to call him her son-in-law.''

"What else? Why were you willing to marry a man you didn't love in order to please your mother?''

"I thought Michael and I could grow to love each other over time. He's well established. He has plans and goals. I thought that's what I needed—a real go-getter. But the longer I'm his secretary, the more I see what an empty life he leads.''

"Empty life?''

"His life has no real meaning. It's filled with tight schedules, constant problems and nothing else.''

"But Sophia, Michael Barrington's a busy guy. He's got lots of employees depending on his leadership. I mean you can't have it both ways. If he's a high achiever he's not going to have a lot of time to spend with his family.''

"That's what I've come to realize. He doesn't get to stop and smell the roses. I feel sorry for Michael. I know he doesn't have a girlfriend and I don't think he's even got any buddies. I mean, look at you. Everyone at Barrington loves you.''

"They do?''

"How could they not? You think about other people. You smile, you're interested. You pitch in without even being asked to help out. You really care about people.

From what I can figure out, Michael Barrington is only interested in acquiring money.''

Mike winced. *Ouch!* The portrait Sophia had painted of him was not flattering.

''You never answered my question, Mike. Are you willing to give up your lifestyle? To settle down and find a real job? Can you do that for me? Because if you can't, all the chemistry in the world is useless.''

''Useless? Tell me this means nothing, Sophia.'' He ran his fingers along the underside of her bare arm, heard her hiss in her breath.

''Mike, I won't be like my mother. I won't jeopardize my future or the future of any children I might conceive for a few moments of passion.''

''I'm not asking you to do that, Sophia.''

''What are you saying?''

How he wished he could see her face, to observe the expression in her eyes when he told her that he loved her. That no woman on the face of the earth had ever moved him the way she did.

''I love you, Sophia, more than you can ever know. I'd do anything to win your heart.'' Words he had not planned to utter poured from somewhere deep inside Mike.

''You'd find a stable and secure job?'' She grasped his hand tightly.

''Yes.''

''We could date a while, really get to know each other before things went any further?''

''Absolutely.''

''You'll be perfectly honest with me?''

''Oh, Sophia…'' He was about to tell her everything.

''Yes, Mike,'' she said. ''It's you I want. Somewhere inside me I've always known it was you from the moment you started to work at Barrington. Nobody had ever been able to move me with just one glance. But you did. I love you, Mike.''

Then Sophia kissed him and he flew straight to heaven.

Sophia had passed his test. She'd chosen poor mailman Mike over rich Michael Barrington. She'd followed her heart instead of her head. She was not, after all, like Erica, who'd only been interested in his money. Sophia Shepherd loved him.

Or did she?

Sophia thought she was getting Mike the mailman. That's who she wanted. The sexy, rugged, motorcycle-riding Mike, not Michael, the busy corporate executive. Doubt gripped him once more.

''Mike,'' she whispered huskily, ''hold me.''

He could not resist her. They melted together. Right there on the floor of the elevator. Neither able to control themselves.

Joy beat through Sophia's heart. *Mike loves me.*

So many nights she dreamed of this moment, when a man would profess his love for her and mean it. Of course she'd often dreamed that man would be Michael Barrington, but she knew that had been an infatuation. The man she really loved was here in her arms. Honest, sincere, good-hearted Mike. Sexy, adventuresome, fun-loving Mike who was willing to give up his transient lifestyle in order to be with her. If that didn't prove he loved her, nothing would.

She buried her head into the curve of his neck and licked his skin, reveling in his salty taste.

The strength of her desire for this man hit her like a punch. She wanted him. Here. Now. In the dark and damn the consequences.

Mike plunged his fingers through her hair. She raised her head and met his lips once more. They burned. Fiery, feverish with wanting. There was no denying his feelings for her. She could feel it in the tension of his corded arm muscles, could taste his love for her on his tongue.

She ached to see his face, to stare into those green eyes and observe her love for him reflected back at her.

Mike groaned low in his throat and Sophia was startled to hear herself making mewling sounds. She sounded like Shu-Shu did when she was being stroked and petted.

"You're so beautiful," he whispered. "Gorgeous."

"You can't even see me." Sophia giggled, wrapping both arms around his neck and clinging to him.

"I know what you look like. In that sexy little outfit you wore to the company picnic, you could raise the dead. I can see it as clearly as if you were dressed in it right now and standing under floodlights."

"You're silly."

"Silly for you." He kissed the tip of her nose.

"I want you, Mike."

"You've got me, Sophia. Forever."

"You really mean that?"

He clicked his tongue, scolding her. "Do you really have to ask?"

"I've just got to know that you're telling me the truth, that if I let you make love to me, it's not the biggest mistake of my life."

"Sophia, I'm not going to make love to you. Not in a stalled elevator without any lights."

"Why not?"

"Believe me, it's not because I don't want to, but our first time should be special."

"This is special," she insisted.

"I don't have any…er…protection."

"A guy like you?" she teased. "According to the office rumors you're always prepared."

"The office rumors are wrong, Sophia." His voice was serious. "I don't give of myself lightly."

Another thrill raced through her at his words. So Mike was not as free and easy with his love as others would have had her believe. She really was special to him.

"But," he said, "there is something I can do for you."

"For me?" Sophia was puzzled.

"Shhh." Softly, slowly, he kissed her again. While his lips kept her mouth busy, his hands were doing some exploring of their own.

He tugged her blouse from the waistband of her skirt and slipped his hand inside. When his palm touched her bare belly, Sophia hissed in air through clenched teeth.

"Oh, Mike."

"Oh, Mike, yes, or oh, Mike, no?"

"Yes," she whimpered, and her temperature shot to the ceiling when she recalled what his mouth had done to her breasts on that long-ago Friday night.

She could feel him grinning.

"That's my girl."

His fingers caressed. They explored and teased. A gentle grazing across her stomach until Sophia thought she'd go insane from sheer pleasure. He barely touched her and yet her nerve endings came alive with sensations. Fine hairs all over her body stood at attention and a field of goose bumps sprouted over her flesh.

Did he do everything this slowly, this deliberately?

The darkness was a cover for her modesty and Sophia appreciated that but the lack of light was also a hindrance. She wanted to see Mike. The expression on his face, the sparkle in his eyes, his knowing grin.

Then his fingers found the hook on her bra and quickly went about setting her free. He was just as gentle with her breasts. Soon Sophia was writhing against him, begging for more, awash in ecstasy.

Her body was completely pliant under his caring touch. The intense throbbing between her thighs swelled until her entire being was engulfed in a power unlike anything she'd experienced.

He unzipped her skirt. His hand delved lower, his fingers tracing a path from her navel to her panties.

Arching her back, she quivered against his touching, anxious to see how far he would go.

"Mike," she begged. "Mike."

He rubbed the outside of her panties, the silken material separating her aching pelvis from his fingers. She wanted more. More!

"Yes, Sophia," he whispered. "Yes."

And it felt so right. So good. So perfect.

His lips crushed hers, his kisses growing harder, firmer, his own desire escalating as she grew more excited.

She tore at his shirt. Buttons popped and scattered across the elevator with a flat sound as they hit.

"Sophia," he groaned, "what are you doing?"

"Getting even," she replied, splaying her hands across his chest.

"No," he said. "Please. I don't know how much longer I can control myself."

"Tough," she replied, and playfully nipped his bottom lip.

The baby quilt beneath them was soft and smelled of cotton. Sophia breathed deeply, inhaling other smells. The scent of love. It was on them, between them. It seeped from their pores and mingled as an erotic, exotic perfume of their own making.

"Sophia," he said, moving abruptly to a sitting position. He grasped both her shoulders in his hands, his fingers digging into her skin. "We must stop."

"Why?" she whispered, getting on her knees to nuzzle his neck. "I love you and you said you loved me. What's wrong with us showing that love?"

"Remember what happened to your mother?"

"But if our lovemaking resulted in a child, you'd marry me, Mike," she said. He did not say anything to reassure her of this. Her stomach lurched. "Right?"

"There's something I must tell you, Sophia. Something that might make a difference in the way you feel about me."

"Mike?" Her voice trembled. "What's wrong? Are you in trouble with the law?"

"No. Listen, I feel like a coward, telling you now, in the dark without being able to see your face, but you've got to know sooner or later."

"Know what?"

His tone scared her. A bubble of hysteria began to build inside Sophia, pressing hard against her rib cage. What could Mike possibly have done that would affect the way she felt about him? A hundred terrible scenarios raced through her head.

Did he use drugs? Did he have a gambling problem? Had he fathered an illegitimate child and abandoned it? Suddenly Sophia realized how little she knew about this man she loved so fiercely.

"Mike," she said, "you're scaring me."

He took a deep breath. His sigh echoed off the metal walls. "I'm just going to come right out and say it."

She groped for his hand. "Whatever problem you've got, Mike, we'll work through it. I'm here for you. I'm not going to withdraw my love simply because you've got a problem."

"Do you mean it, Sophia?"

"Yes."

"You say that now...."

"I'm serious. Please, just don't lie to me."

"That's exactly what I've been doing, Sophia."

"What do you mean?" Alarm spread through her as

destructive as an earthquake, rattling the foundation of her beliefs.

"I've lied to everyone."

"Everyone? What are you talking about?" Confusion clouded her mind, dissipating the intense ardor she'd experienced a few short minutes earlier.

"I'm a liar and worse."

"Worse?" She clasped a hand to her chest.

"I'm a spy."

A spy? Sophia furrowed her brow. "I don't understand."

"I'm not who you think I am."

"You're not Mike Barr the office mailman?"

"No."

Had the bottom dropped out of the elevator? Was she free-falling through an abyss? What was happening to her? One minute she was in utopia, being kissed and held by the man she loved, the next minute he was telling her she didn't even known him at all.

"Who are you?" she asked softly.

"Why, haven't you guessed by now?"

"No." She had no idea what he was talking about.

"Think about it, Sophia. Who do I sound like?" His voice suddenly changed. Gone was the slow, seductive drawl and in its place was the firm, commanding tones of her boss.

"Oh, no," she gasped, and plastered a palm across her mouth.

"Yes," he said grimly. "I'm Rex Michael Barrington III."

Chapter Eleven

He had lied to her!

The ramifications of his statement sledgehammered Sophia. Over the past few months that she had been working for him, thinking he was away in Germany, he'd been right here under her nose the whole time. Watching her. Spying on her. Leading her on.

He'd seen her romantic doodlings, Sophia realized. He'd heard her tell Olivia she was going to marry him. She'd told him she felt sorry for him and the empty life he lead.

Shame burned her cheeks.

Well, she rationalized, hadn't he asked for it by hiding his true identity? By sneaking around, hadn't Michael Barrington laid himself open to hearing unflattering things? She had no reason to be ashamed.

Other thoughts flashed through her mind. The motorcycle ride, the night he'd stayed late and ordered pizza. He'd told her he was coming to the company picnic and had instead shown up as Mike. No doubt he'd rigged the three-legged race in order to be teamed with her.

Of all the audacity! Was everything about this conniving man a lie? What about his profession of love? Was that a lie, as well?

Anger quickly replaced her embarrassment. His behavior was unbelievable, not to mention unethical.

"You...you..." Sophia sputtered, unable to think of the appropriate word to describe what he had done.

Then suddenly the lights came on, dashing them in blinding illumination.

Sophia blinked. She was still on her knees, clutching both hands into tight fists.

The baby quilt was wadded up beneath them. Her purse and the paper sack lay strewn to one side. Mike. No *Michael* was sitting only inches in front of her, his hair in disarray, the buttons missing from his shirt, her lipstick imprints adorning his cheek and chin.

"I'm sorry, Sophia," he said. "I never meant for things to turn out this way." He got to his feet, held his hand out to her.

But she was having none of it. Sophia pushed aside his hand and struggled to stand. An apology would not right the wrong he had committed, nor would it mend her broken heart.

In her book, Michael Barrington had committed the ultimate sin. He had lied to her. As her father had lied to her mother. How could she ever hope to trust this man again?

Sophia swallowed hard and glanced away. She couldn't bear to look at him. Didn't dare consider that she had almost made love to him.

Her mother had been right from the beginning. Men weren't to be trusted. They were dirty, low-down, lying snakes! And Michael Barrington was king snake of them all.

She was breathing hard. Her blouse was unbuttoned. Her

bra hung unhooked, her skirt twisted. With trembling hands, she reached to repair her clothing.

Sophia registered the sound of a whirling engine. The elevator had come to life.

In that moment the door slid open.

She and Michael stared out to find Rex Barrington, Mildred Van Hess, Sophia's mother and Stanley Whitcomb staring back.

"Sophia?" Her mother knocked lightly on her bedroom door. "Are you all right?"

"I don't want to talk about it." Sophia sniffled into her pillow.

"Honey, please let me come in. I hate to see you hurting this way."

"You're just going to say I told you so."

"Sophia, really, do you think I'm that heartless?"

Sighing, Sophia got off the bed and went to unlock her bedroom door. Her mother wheeled into the room, concern etching wrinkles across her forehead. She held out her arms. Sophia sank to her knees in front of the wheelchair and allowed her mother to cradle her against her chest.

"It'll be okay, baby," Jannette soothed, patting Sophia's hair. "I promise."

"You were right," Sophia said. "Mike did cause me trouble."

"Listen, sweetie, don't be ashamed. It could happen to anyone. Getting trapped for hours in an elevator with a man who generates such passion in you would make the strongest woman lose her head. No one would blame you."

Startled, Sophia pulled back and looked at Jannette. "Are you my mother?"

"I know, it's an about-face for me."

"That's an understatement. For my entire life you've

been predicting dire happenings if I let my heart rule my head, if I went for passion above security. What's mellowed you?''

A modest smile curled the corner of her lips. ''Ever since I met Stanley Whitcomb, I've been doing a lot of thinking lately. He's such a sensible man. Honest and sincere. I've never met anyone quite like him.''

''Mom!'' Sophia stared. ''What are you saying?''

Jannette waved a hand. ''Don't jump to conclusions, honey. Stanley and I are just friends. But he's the first man I've felt comfortable talking to in my entire life. That's pretty sad when you're forty-six years old. I've let bitterness rule my life for too long. I've allowed your father to color my whole outlook toward men. I hurt myself and I harmed you in the process.''

''Mom, you don't know how long I've waited to hear you say that.'' Sophia squeezed Jannette tightly. ''Are you sure this thing between you and Stanley is strictly platonic? You have a lot to offer, if you'd just let yourself.''

''It's too soon to speculate on that. Let's simply say I've got a new friend.''

''I'm happy for you. Stanley is a great guy.''

Jannette smiled shyly. ''Yes, he is, but what's all this about Mike actually being Michael Barrington?''

''It's true,'' Sophia said glumly. ''He went undercover as the mailman, spying on the employees.''

''Sounds like a cagey move to me. Checking out the inner workings of the company before taking over.''

''Mom! He's a liar.''

''Do you love him?''

''I don't know anymore. He's not the man I thought he was.''

''You're twenty-nine years old, Sophia. You can make your own mistakes now.''

"Boy," Sophia said regretfully. "When I make them, I make them big."

"I was wrong in the way I raised you," Jannette said. "I was much too harsh."

"Sometimes you were." Sophia chuckled. "I still remember the first guy I ever went out with."

"Chuck Clark." Jannette smiled. "He had red hair and ears like a stop sign."

"But I had a huge crush on him."

"I know." Jannette raised her eyebrows. "I was terrified you were going to let him kiss you. Remember, I was only a year older than you were then when I got into trouble."

"You told Chuck if he didn't have me home by ten o'clock you'd come after him with a hatchet."

"I was bad, wasn't I?"

"He never asked me out again."

"I'm so sorry, Sophia. I let my mistakes ruin your childhood." Jannette stroked her hand.

"Oh, Mom, my childhood was fine."

"Really?"

"We might not have had a lot of things, but I always knew you loved me."

"I did love you so much. You'll never know how much until you have children of your own." Tears misted Jannette's eyes.

Sophia kissed her mother's cheek. "Thank you," she said, "for understanding."

"So what are you going to do about Mike?"

"There's no way I can continue to work for him."

Misery gnawed a hole through her gut. She still loved Mike. No matter how deceitful he might have been, she could not forget the feelings he stirred in her. But how could she continue to work for a dishonest man? How could she even consider a future with him? A man who lacked the most basic of admirable qualities—honesty.

"But you love your job," Jannette protested.

"There are other jobs."

"Are you sure about this? Take your time. Think it over. There's no rush."

"Mom, I have no choice. I simply can't be around Michael. Tomorrow, I'm turning in my resignation."

He'd blown it.

Big-time.

Actually, a nuclear bomb would have done less damage than the graceless way he'd revealed his true identity to Sophia. He'd handled the situation so poorly, he doubted she'd ever speak to him again, much less give him another opportunity.

He should have told her sooner. It had been a mistake to wait so long. But before he could tell her he was Michael Barrington, he had to know she loved him and not his money. So he'd waited, too afraid to take a chance. Now it was unlikely she'd forgive him for deceiving her.

Sophia had been hurt and he could not fault her response. He was a liar and a sneak. He had been spying on his employees. People who had come to like and trust Mike the mailman. What would be their reaction tomorrow morning when the truth came out? Most of them would feel betrayed and taken advantage of.

Mike drove his motorcycle through the Arizona night, the warm arid winds rippling over his skin. It was three o'clock in the morning and he'd been riding since leaving the building after that embarrassing episode in the elevator.

He saw now that his charade had been wrong. It didn't matter that his intentions had been the best. He'd simply wanted to make sure that the Barrington Corporation was in tip-top shape. It pained him to know he'd injured Sophia in the process.

Swallowing against the fierce ache that enveloped not only his entire body but his psyche, as well, Mike revved the engine and spurred the motorcycle faster down the desert road, his headlights cutting a thin slice of light through the darkness.

He hadn't felt such emotional pain since he'd lost his mother to breast cancer. And although his mother's death had been profoundly sad, that loss had been beyond his control. This matter with Sophia however, was a disaster of his own making. He had no one else to blame but himself.

As a businessman, he was accustomed to taking calculated risks and having them pay off. When he'd decided to win her over as Mike the mailman, he had known that the dangers involved not only losing his own heart, but breaking hers in the process. He'd taken the gamble and failed. Miserably.

That's what upset him most. Breaking her heart. Sophia was such a tender, loving person. She deserved to be cherished, treated with the utmost love and respect. Instead, he'd toyed with her affections in order to assure his emotional survival.

It was not an attractive thing to admit about himself. In his insecurity, he had damaged the woman he loved more than any other.

His inability to trust had caused his downfall. His father had been right all along.

That's it, Barrington? A voice that sounded an awful lot like Mike the mailman whispered at the back of his mind. *You're going to give up just like that?*

"What can I do?" Michael growled under his breath. "She doesn't want me."

She told you she loved you.

"No." Mike laughed harshly at the yellow half-moon dangling in the sky above. "She loves Mike the mailman."

Ironically he was caught in a trap of his own making. He'd wanted her to fall in love with Mike. To prove that she could follow her heart and let herself care for a poor man.

He had succeeded only too well. Now she was in love with the man she believed him to be, but Michael was not like that image. He was not footloose and fancy-free. He did not have scores of friends. He was not fun and adventuresome. He was not low-key and easygoing.

Sophia was correct in her assessment of him. He did lead an empty life. In the aftermath of his mother's death and Erica's manipulations, he'd focused all his energies on work. Making his way in the corporate world, proving to himself and his father that he was not the rebellious spoiled brat he had once been had become his main goals. He did not stop to smell the roses.

But you could change, the voice insisted. *Part of you is Mike the mailman. Part of you aches to let down your guard and learn to trust. Part of you wants to kick up your heels, have a good time and love. Truly love without any reservations or hesitations.*

Hope flickered inside him. Maybe he could convince Sophia to give him a second chance.

There was only one way to find out.

Making a U-turn, Michael headed the Harley for home.

At eight o'clock the following morning, Mike walked into the employee break room with the intention of grabbing a cup of coffee to fortify himself before calling a company meeting and announcing the official arrival of Rex Michael Barrington III.

"Surprise!"

Stunned, Michael stared.

It seemed the entire building was in attendance. The place was packed with at least three dozen people sporting party hats and brandishing noisemakers. He spotted all his friends. Jack and Nick. Sam and Lucas. Kyle and Cindy. Stanley Whitcomb. Rachel and Patricia and Molly. On the wall behind the coffeemaker was a large banner proclaiming We'll Miss You, Mike. A multilayered chocolate cake sat on the table spelling out Farewell, Mike in cream frosting.

A lump formed in his throat.

Ah, jeez. He'd never expected this. A going-away party.

The fact that he was about to reveal his true identity and shatter their confidence was not lost on Michael. Swallowing hard, he searched the crowd for Sophia.

She was nowhere to be seen.

"Hey, buddy." Jack stepped forward to slap him on the back. "You sure look surprised."

"I am."

"Come on in," Cindy invited, ushering him across the threshold. "Have a piece of cake."

"It's going to be awfully lonesome around here without you," Sam said.

"We got you a present," Nick offered, holding up shiny new handlebars for his motorcycle, a bright red bow tied around them. "We don't want you to forget us."

Guilt heaped on more guilt. Overwhelmed by their generosity, Michael could say nothing. He was moved forward by the crowd and took the handlebars Nick thrust into his hands.

"I...I can't accept this," he said.

The door opened and Michael turned his head. Sophia entered the room, her arms crossed over her chest, her blue eyes flashing with anger. He'd never seen anything so beautiful, so sexy and inspiring in his entire life. He had to tell everyone. Here. Now. With Sophia as witness.

"Don't be silly," Jack said. "We got them just for you."

"It's our way of showing how much we love you, Mike," Patricia Peel said.

For the first time, he realized that it was true. He was beloved by his co-workers. And he'd betrayed their trust.

Michael locked eyes with Sophia, searching for her reaction. Bravely she did not flinch or blink.

"I can't accept your generous gift for two reasons." He cleared his throat and spoke firmly, vaguely aware of the people separating him from Sophia. "First, I'm not quitting."

A shout of glee went up from his audience. "That's great," several people commented.

"We knew you couldn't leave us," someone shouted.

"You can keep the gift anyway," Nick insisted. "As a token of our esteem."

"When I finish what I've got to say," Michael replied soberly. "I hope I still have your esteem."

Everyone quieted. They looked from him to Sophia and back again. The tension was unmistakable.

He longed to take her into his arms, to block out what was happening, to declare his love for her in front of everyone. He ached to kiss those lips, to run his fingers through those gorgeous blond curls, to hold her tightly and never let her go.

Momentarily breaking eye contact with Sophia, Michael glanced around the room at his friends and co-workers. "I've got an announcement to make."

No one spoke. He took a deep breath. He had instigated this charade; only he could end it.

"I'm your new boss. Rex Michael Barrington III."

Sophia's gut torqued. Painfully, miserably. Every time Mike uttered those telling words, it was a fresh blow to her heart. Now, hearing him say it again made her realize she was doing the right thing.

In her purse sat her resignation letter.

Final and conclusive. Declaring that her work for the Barrington Corporation was at an end.

Tears collected at the corners of her eyes. Determined not to let Mike see her cry, she spun on her heel and raced from the break room.

''Excuse me,'' she heard him tell the group.

He was coming after her!

Pulse pushing against her veins, urging her faster, Sophia bolted down the hallway.

''Sophia!''

His shoes slapped against the tile, echoing in the corridor.

Should she run for her office or the safety of the parking lot? In her office, she'd be cornered. The parking lot offered a clean getaway.

But no matter how tempting the parking lot might be, she couldn't run away from this. No matter what other faults she might possess, Sophia was not a coward. Sooner or later she had to face him.

Abruptly she stopped outside the elevators. The very elevator where they had been so intimately trapped the night before. The elevator where she'd discovered the truth—that the man she loved was a deceitful liar, accustomed to manipulating people for his own purposes. Exactly the sort of man Jannette had warned her about.

She forced herself to breathe slowly.

''Sophia!''

Calmly she extracted the envelope from her purse and turned to face him. Schooling her features to reveal a disinterest she did not feel, Sophia raised her chin.

''Good morning, Mr. Barrington.''

''Sophia, we've got to talk.''

He looked so sad, so disheveled with his hair mussed and his tie askew that Sophia had to bite her lip to bolster her resolve. She could not allow his apparent vulnerability to sway her. This man was not what he appeared to be. On any level.

"There's nothing left to say." She handed him the envelope.

"What's this?"

"Read it."

Mike tore open the envelope, scanned the words. "Sophia," he said. "You can't quit your job over me."

"It's a free country." She tossed her head, prayed her voice would not crack from the weight of her emotions. "I can do anything I wish."

"You need your job to support your mother."

"Don't worry about us. We'll survive."

"Please," Michael said. "I know things will probably never be right between you and I, but you can't quit. You're too good an employee. Losing you would be a grave blow to Barrington."

"No one's irreplaceable. Especially me. You'll find someone else," she said.

How much effort it took for her to stare into those green eyes and remain solidly committed to her course of action! She wanted to forgive him, but how could she? If he would lie to her about his very identity, he would lie to her about anything. She simply could not be with a man she could not trust.

"I understand that you no longer feel comfortable as my secretary but that doesn't mean you can't continue to work for the company."

She had loved working here, had made many friends. It would be hard to leave. "Michael, I can no longer even remain in the same building with you. Not after the way you tricked me. It would be too painful."

"Sophia, I'm so sorry." Michael reached out for her but she shied away.

"No."

There was no mistaking the hurt in his eyes. He nodded. "I understand."

From down the hall, Sophia could see several people poking their heads out of the break room. This was turning into a circus.

"I could recommend you to one of our other branches," Mike offered. "Say, the office in Sedona."

"Unfortunately my answer is still no. Please consider my resignation effective immediately."

Unable to speak another word to the man who had so completely destroyed her world, Sophia turned and fled.

Chapter Twelve

"Sophia," her mother called out to her, "there's someone here to see you."

Michael! Her heart leapt with joy then just as quickly plummeted. For the last three days her spirits had ridden this wild roller coaster ride, one moment hopeful for the future, the next in deep despair for what she had lost. But she was not going back to work for him.

Sophia opened her bedroom door. "I don't want to see anyone."

"It's not Michael," her mother said.

"Oh. Just a minute."

She darted to the bathroom to put on some lipstick. Her eyes were puffy and red from crying. She'd never been so miserable. How long would it take for the hurt and betrayal to dissipate? How long before she could sleep at night? How long before she could eat more than a few bites at mealtimes? How long before she stopped seeing Michael Barrington's face every time she closed her eyes? How long before she forgot about his kisses, the feel of his hands on her skin?

Taking a deep breath, Sophia forced herself to go into the living room and greet her guest. To her surprise, she found Mildred Van Hess sitting on the sofa chatting with her mother.

"Hello, Sophia," Mildred replied in her no-nonsense voice.

"Nice to see you."

"I'll leave you two alone," Jannette said, and wheeled from the room.

"Have a seat." Mildred patted the cushion beside her.

Tentatively Sophia sat down. "Did Michael send you?"

"No, he did not. He has no idea I'm here but I wanted you to see this letter of recommendation he wrote for your files."

"Mildred," Sophia said. "This isn't going to change my mind about anything."

"Please, just read it."

Hesitantly Sophia took the folded paper Mildred passed to her. Her fingers shook slightly as she opened it and began to read.

To Whom It May Concern,
For the past two years, Sophia Shepherd has been in the employment of the Barrington Corporation. Her work has been excellent, her organizational skills are impeccable. Ms. Shepherd is kind, considerate, hard-working and dedicated. But most of all, she is a very moral person who holds herself and others to the highest standards. She is trustworthy, honorable, open and sincere. In the past five and a half months as my assistant, she has taught me an immeasurable amount about people. Most of all, I have learned from her the importance of honesty. She will be sorely missed at Barrington and by me personally.
Sincerely,
Rex Michael Barrington III

Tears burned the back of her eyelids but Sophia willed them not to trickle down her cheeks and soil the paper. She'd never read such a glowing recommendation letter. And all the personal stuff! How she'd taught him the importance of honesty.

"It came as quite a shock to most of the employees when they learned that Michael and Mike were one and the same," Mildred said.

"I'm sure everyone felt deceived and spied upon."

"Some yes. Others were glad to have a boss so interested in the inner workings of the corporation. Michael apologized for his deception. He realizes now it was the wrong approach. He's changed, Sophia. Because of you."

"I'm not sure I believe that."

"He's lost without you," Mildred said. "When I come into the office in the mornings, I catch him staring out the window with the saddest expression on his face. He sits like that for hours. He won't take calls and he cancels appointments. Rex simply can't retire as long as Michael is like this."

Mildred's words tore at her heart. "I'm sorry for that," Sophia murmured.

"Maybe if you knew more about Michael's background you would understand better why he did what he did."

"You don't have to make excuses for him, Mildred."

"I'm not making excuses, Sophia. I'm giving you the facts."

"All right," Sophia said. She leaned back against the sofa and waited for Rex Barrington's longtime secretary to continue.

"The Barringtons weren't always wealthy. In fact, at one time they were very poor. But Rex had dreams and ambitions. When Michael was five years old, Rex bought

his first hotel and he moved the family from St. Louis to
Los Angeles. Over the years there were twelve more
moves until they finally headquartered the business in
Phoenix.''

Sophia listened. In her mind's eye she could see Michael
at age five. She imagined that even then he possessed a
killer grin.

''Michael had a hard time leaving his grandparents and
home behind. As a boy he was quite shy and did not make
friends easily. Rex was gone so much, he rarely saw him.
Michael became very close to his mother.''

Sounds like me as a kid, Sophia thought, surprised to
discover her upbringing had not been so different from
Michael's.

''Soon the business mushroomed and Rex became
wealthy beyond his wildest dreams. He showered gifts and
toys on Michael to make up for not being there for him.''

''He must have felt abandoned by his father.''

''Yes. Rex missed so much of Michael's early years. He
didn't attend baseball games or spelling bees. He missed
birthday parties and Boy Scout meetings. He was too busy
building his empire. To Rex, amassing money for his son's
future was more important than playing catch with him in
the backyard. It was only later that he realized what precious moments he'd lost.''

Money. It was as much of a problem as a solution. For
the first time in her life, Sophia realized she had something
money could never buy. Her mother's constant love and
attention.

''Kids wanted to be Michael's friend just to come over
and play with all his stuff. It wasn't long before Michael
began distrusting everyone's motives,'' Mildred continued.
''Then, when he was a teenager, Michael rebelled. He re-
nounced his name. Said he was tired of being loved for
his money and nothing else. He and Rex had a big argu-

ment and Michael took off on his motorcycle. He bummed around for a few years and then he met Erica.''

''Who was she?''

''A scheming little gold digger. But Michael didn't realize she knew who he was and had set herself up to marry him. He fell deeply in love.''

''What happened?'' Sophia asked, her chest squeezing tight. It did explain a lot. Why Michael had gone undercover in his own company. Why he had thought *her* a gold digger. Why he hadn't trusted her enough to let her get to know the real Michael Barrington.

''Michael eventually found out and broke off the engagement. At about the same time, his mother developed cancer. It was heartbreaking.'' Mildred cleared her throat and blinked. ''His mother made Michael promise to mend fences with Rex and to come back home. He did it, of course. I suppose he decided that since he'd lost everything he'd ever loved, he might as well throw himself into the business. It helped him deal with his grief, but it hurt him, too. He's kept himself buried in work for too long.''

''Thank you for telling me this. I do understand Michael better now, but it doesn't change anything. Honesty is very important to me. Michael lied.''

''Are you really so unforgiving?''

Mildred's question took her by surprise. ''I…'' Was it true? Was she like Jannette, holding a grudge when she should be forgiving?

''Michael is such a good man,'' Mildred continued. ''He's got so much love inside him, he's just afraid to give it. That's why he's always driven himself so hard. To avoid his emotions. I think he feels if he ever slows down, he'll realize how empty his life has become. He needs you, Sophia. More than you can ever know. Give him another chance. For both your sakes.''

Mildred's plea touched her. Sophia had never heard the

stoic executive secretary beg anyone for anything. She wasn't making the request for herself. She was doing it for Michael. .

"I don't know." How she wanted to say yes! But she couldn't get her hopes up only to have them dashed again. It hurt too much to hope.

"At least talk to him, Sophia. What could it hurt? He knows he's in the wrong, but he fears you'll reject him if he comes to you. Go to him, Sophia. Forgive."

Sophia could barely contain her grin as she slipped into the outfit she'd rented at a costume store. It was a facsimile of a U.S. postal service uniform. Her heart thudded a mile a minute. She changed clothes in the ladies' rest room in the lobby of the Barrington building. Pulling the cap down low on her brow, she picked up a large cardboard box that weighed only a few ounces and carried it to hide her face.

Taking deep breaths to calm her jangled nerves, Sophia took the elevator to the fifth floor. The same elevator where she and Mike spent their last night together. She glanced at the floor, recalled their passionate embrace. The memory washed over her, increasing the size of the knot in her stomach.

She was scared. Very scared. Going out on a limb for love wasn't for cowards.

But she did love Michael. And Mike! She loved both sides of him. The hardworking, sensible provider and the fun-loving, motorcycle-riding wild man.

She got off the elevator and walked past Mildred's desk.

"Wait just a minute, miss, you can't go in there." Guard dog that she was, Mildred got to her feet.

Sophia turned, met Mildred's steady gaze and winked. The look of surprise crossing her face was quickly replaced with delight.

"Go right on in," Mildred said, struggling to control her smile.

Shouldering the package higher, completely blocking her face from Michael's view, Sophia pushed open the door to his office. She peeked around the package.

His chair was swiveled facing the window and his back was to her. He cradled the back of his head with his palms, his elbows poking out. She lowered the box a little.

"Package for Michael Barrington," she said in a slow drawl, trying hard to imitate the voice he'd used while playing the role of Mike the mailman.

"Set it on the table," he said without even turning around.

"You need to sign for it."

"That's what my secretary is for," he snapped.

"I didn't see any secretary."

"Oh, for crying out loud." Michael sighed. "Mildred." He spun in the chair and got to his feet.

She moved toward him. He still hadn't looked her in the face.

"Give it here." He reached for the package.

Her mouth went suddenly dry. Her breath hung in her lungs. Sudden doubt filled her. What if her ruse angered him?

Don't be ridiculous, she chided herself. Sophia had never seen him get angry, in either of his incarnations. Still, she felt self-conscious and uncertain.

His fingertips grazed her hand as he relieved her of the package. Awareness shot through Sophia like an electrical shock.

"Hey," he said lightly.

"Yes?" Her heart jerked.

"This box is awfully light."

That's when he finally looked at her face. Sophia lifted her lowered lashes to meet his gaze. Those familiar green eyes pinned her to the spot. Her hands trembled with excitement and anticipation.

"Sophia," Michael whispered, and dropped the box on his desk.

Sophia grinned and adjusted her hat. "No," she said. "I'm Sally the mail gal."

His grin matched hers. "Mail gal?"

"Yes. But don't get used to me. I'm footloose and fancy-free. Never in one place very long."

"Hmm." Michael stroked his chin with a thumb and index finger. "I'm not sure I believe you. You look a lot like my old assistant, Sophia Shepherd."

Sophia waved her hand. "Oh, her? No, she's gone forever. Too judgmental. Too unforgiving."

Could it be? Mike asked himself. Had Sophia returned to give him another chance? Hope leapt in his chest.

He reached out and took both her hands in his and drew her close. "Let's see if we can find out what happened to my Sophia." Gently he removed her hat. Blond curls tumbled free, cascading about her shoulders. She was so beautiful, it took his breath. And the comical way she'd dressed in a postal uniform—how clever.

"You look like Sophia."

"I'm not. She's too insecure."

"No, she's tough and strong. A girl who has her principles and sticks to them."

"To her own detriment."

"Let's see if you taste like Sophia." Enjoying the game they were playing, Michael hooked a finger under her chin and tilted her face. Tentatively he lowered his head and brushed his lips across hers. Instantly, sparks flared.

Ah. Chemistry.

"You taste like Sophia."

"Coincidence." She breathed heavily, assuring him she felt as much desire as he did.

Michael buried his nose in the curve of her neck, smelled the scent of sunflowers. "You smell like Sophia."

"A common perfume."

"So you're telling me you're a completely different person?"

"Absolutely. I don't care what kind of job a man has as long as he loves me."

"Really?" Michael scarcely dared to draw in air. What was Sophia saying?

"Really."

"Oh, Sophia." He crushed her to his chest, then rained kisses on her eyelids, her nose, her cheeks. "You don't know how I've longed to hear you say those words. Tell me the truth. What made you change your mind and come back?"

"Mildred," Sophia said. "She showed me the letter of recommendation you wrote. She told me about your childhood, the things that formed you. That's when I began to understand."

"Understand what?"

"That you were only trying to protect your heart. You were afraid of getting hurt. Of marrying someone who didn't love you. But I love you, Michael. Both sides of you."

"Oh, sweetheart, I love you more than words can say. Thank you for saving me from myself. Because of you I took a long hard look at myself. You were right. I did lead an empty life."

"You just wanted to succeed."

"No, I used success as a cop-out. I made it the most important thing in my life when people are what should have been taking center stage. You showed me so much, Sophia. Because of you, I've learned honesty is the best policy. I've learned to trust people until they prove themselves unworthy of my trust, not the other way around."

"You taught me a few things, too."

"Oh, yeah?" He smiled.

"Yeah."

"Like what?"

"You can't judge a book by its cover."

He nodded.

"But I learned something even more important."

"What's that?"

"Money can't buy happiness. Work can't buy security. Things can't buy safety. Only love and belief in yourself can bring peace of mind."

"We've got enough love to buy a lifetime of happiness," Michael said softly. "You and me."

"Yes."

"Are you willing to put up with me for a very long time to come?" He brushed a lock of hair from her eyes.

"What are you asking?"

Effervescent bubbles foamed inside her. Everything she'd ever wanted was coming true. She had a man who loved her. A man who would stick by her through thick and thin. A man who would put his love for his family before everything else.

"I love you, Sophia. Will you marry me?"

"Look inside the box."

"There's an answer in the package?"

"Open it and see."

With one hand around her waist, Michael leaned over and stripped the heavy brown tape from the box. He flipped back the lid and peered inside. His laughter filled the room as he grabbed handfuls of notes and tossed them in the air.

A hundred slips of paper fluttered around them, drifting slowly to the floor. Written on each and every one were the words *Mrs. Rex Michael Barrington III.*

Epilogue

"Do you, Sophia Denise Shepherd, take this man to be your lawfully wedded husband?"

The words Sophia had waited a lifetime to hear rang joyfully in her ears. The scent of roses and orchids wafted up from her bouquet, enveloping them in a heavenly aroma. Trembling, she squeezed Michael's hand and their gazes melded. Looking deep into his dark green eyes she saw love so pure and lasting that tears threatened to stream down her face.

"I do." She spoke clearly, no uncertainty in her voice.

For she had found her place at last in the arms of a man who truly loved her. He was everything she had ever wanted, and more. So much more! Nothing could compare with the happiness surging through her chest, filling her with warmth that promised to linger throughout the years ahead. Through bad times and in good. Through sickness and in health. She knew that no matter what happened, she could always count on Michael, for both fun and stability, to provide financially for their future children and to meet their emotional needs. Together they would find a happy balance between work and play. Together they would create the best marriage ever. One born of chemistry and attraction. One based on love and mutual respect. One nurtured on honesty and trust.

"I now pronounce you man and wife. You may kiss the bride."

And then Michael was kissing her, in front of all their friends and family to the accompaniment of cheers and applause.

Be careful what you wish for, you just might get it. Sophia smiled to herself. She had gotten her heart's most deepest desire. She'd found true love.

As they left the church, Sophia paused on the steps to throw the bouquet. She saw her friends gathered, her mother and Stanley arm in arm. Olivia and Lucas with six-month-old Nathaniel. Cindy and Kyle. Patricia and Sam. Molly and Jack. Rachel and Nick. Almost all her friends at the Barrington Corporation were married, each woman having achieved her goal of wedding her boss. Everyone that is, except one.

Sophia caught Mildred's eye. Winking broadly, she tossed her the bouquet.

Deftly Mildred snagged it. Blushing, she turned to show her prize to her boss, Rex Barrington.

"Looks like my father is headed down the aisle." Michael chuckled near Sophia's ear.

"He and Mildred both deserve to be happy."

"As do we," he said, taking her arm.

They reached the bottom of the steps and Sophia was surprised to see the Harley-Davidson parked beside a stretch limousine.

"Which shall it be tonight, darling? Michael and champagne or Mike and beer?"

"On our wedding night? Do you even need to ask?"

Michael grinned. He didn't have to ask. He knew his bride as well as he knew his own name.

With a parting farewell, they climbed aboard the motorcycle and drove off into their very bright and happy future.

*   *   *   *   *

*Be sure to look for the
next book from Laura Anthony.
Don't miss THE TWENTY-FOUR-HOUR GROOM,
available in September
from Silhouette Romance.*

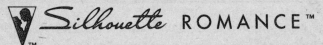

If you enjoyed what you just read,
then we've got an offer you can't resist!

Take 2 bestselling
love stories FREE!

Plus get a FREE surprise gift!

Clip this page and mail it to Silhouette Reader Service™

IN U.S.A.	IN CANADA
3010 Walden Ave.	P.O. Box 609
P.O. Box 1867	Fort Erie, Ontario
Buffalo, N.Y. 14240-1867	L2A 5X3

YES! Please send me 2 free Silhouette Romance® novels and my free surprise gift. Then send me 6 brand-new novels every month, which I will receive months before they're available in stores. In the U.S.A., bill me at the bargain price of $2.90 plus 25¢ delivery per book and applicable sales tax, if any*. In Canada, bill me at the bargain price of $3.25 plus 25¢ delivery per book and applicable taxes**. That's the complete price and a savings of over 10% off the cover prices—what a great deal! I understand that accepting the 2 free books and gift places me under no obligation ever to buy any books. I can always return a shipment and cancel at any time. Even if I never buy another book from Silhouette, the 2 free books and gift are mine to keep forever. So why not take us up on our invitation. You'll be glad you did!

215 SEN CNE7
315 SEN CNE9

Name	(PLEASE PRINT)	
Address	Apt.#	
City	State/Prov.	Zip/Postal Code

* Terms and prices subject to change without notice. Sales tax applicable in N.Y.
** Canadian residents will be charged applicable provincial taxes and GST.
  All orders subject to approval. Offer limited to one per household.
  ® are registered trademarks of Harlequin Enterprises Limited.

SROM99   ©1998 Harlequin Enterprises Limited

Silhouette ROMANCE™
twins on the doorstep

STELLA BAGWELL

continues her wonderful stories of the Murdocks
in Romance & *Special Edition!*

MILLIONAIRE ON HER DOORSTEP—May 1999
(SR#1368)

Then be sure to follow this miniseries when it
leaps into Silhouette Special Edition® with
Sheriff Ethan Hamilton, the son of Rose and
Harlan. Discover what happens when a small
New Mexico town finds out that...

PENNY PARKER'S PREGNANT!—July 1999
(SE#1258)

Judge Penny Parker longed to be a mother, but
the lonely judge needed more than the sheriff's
offer of a "trial" marriage....

Look for a new Murdocks short story in
Silhouette's Mother's Day collection, coming out in
May 2000

Available at your favorite retail outlet.

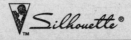

Silhouette®